■ ■ ■ ■ ■ ■ ■ ■ ■ ■ ■ ■ ■ ■

Dr. Patchwork, clad in a one-piece vendorsuit, was standing next to a soydog cart and pretending to solicit the few patrons who were leaving the domed playhouse. Jake, the wardrobe trunk on one shoulder, said, "Pace proved to be a tough opponent. It was nip and tuck there for a spell."

"Dump him in the van and we'll be off for Anaheim," said the doctor. "We may use Pace's parts to build the new team of improved Patchwork Men. The ones I intend to use to take control of the Ladies Mafia once that dippy redhead's established it. I've been ignored and maligned too long by the so-called powers that be and now, since fate has seen fit to send me a little capital, my day is dawning. Keep a man of genius on the outside looking in, my friends, and I warn you, he will one fine day break in! Yes, into your highclass parlors and your. . . ."

■ ■ ■ ■ ■ ■ ■ ■ ■ ■ ■ ■ ■ ■

Calling
Dr. Patchwork

Ron Goulart

DAW BOOKS, INC.

DONALD A. WOLLHEIM, PUBLISHER

1301 Avenue of the Americas
New York, N. Y.   10019

Published by
THE NEW AMERICAN LIBRARY
OF CANADA LIMITED

First Printing, March 1978

1 2 3 4 5 6 7 8 9

PRINTED IN CANADA
COVER PRINTED IN U.S.A.

Chapter 1

————◆————

This particular attempt to kill them came as a surprise.

Well, not a complete surprise since the Great Lando was hinting at it from the amphitheater stage when the man with the flame-hand made his try.

Let's backtrack and orient ourselves. It's a crisp clean autumn day in the year 2002 and we're in the New Westport Vaudeville Amphitheater, which is, as you probably know, built on stilts out over the barely polluted waters of Long Island Sound. The theater holds 900 people and is full this afternoon, probably because a percentage of the profits is going to the Republican-Democrat Party election committee. But then, vaudeville has been drawing good crowds since the turn of the century.

Jake Pace is a long lean man of thirty-six, tanned and capable-looking. His wife, Hildy, is a very attractive red-haired woman of thirty-two. Five feet ten, she is frequently described as willowy. She and Jake, holding hands, were sitting in row J of the second tier on this afternoon.

Up on the floating boomerang-shaped stage the Great Lando, a very small black man in a one-piece scarlet neosilk magic suit and matching cloak, was in the midst of his mentalist act. He stood crouched on the stage rim, pointing at the second row of the first tier and a matronly woman in a pearl dress. "It is a missing brooch which is troubling you," he said. "A baker's dozen of blood-red rubies in a gold setting, framed in square-cut diamonds."

"Oh, blimey, yes," gasped the plump woman as she pressed her ringed fingers against her bosom. "It's lost, misplaced."

"How could you misplace something like that?" Hildy asked with lips close to Jake's ear. "It must glow in the dark."

"Hush, no heckling. I'm curious about this guy."

"I'm not heckling him. I'm heckling you if anybody."

Jake gave her one of his slightly grim smiles and leaned forward, resting his bony hands on the tubular back of the empty chair in front of him.

"The brooch you seek is—I see it glowing!"

"Told you it glowed," said Hildy.

"Yes, I see whereat you may find the missing . . . Holy Christ!" The Great Lando doubled up, clutching at his stomach. "A man with a flaming hand . . . He is here . . . Death! He brings death!"

"What's that got to do with me blinking brooch?" the matron demanded.

"Odd jobs . . . odd jobs," muttered the mentalist. "He . . . wants to kill them . . ."

"Hey!" Jake jumped up. "That must be us."

"Down, sit down, you!"

Ignoring the selectman in the chair directly behind him, Jake rapidly scanned the audience around them.

"I knew we were in for trouble sitting so near them," remarked a Chinese neopath a few seats over.

"Don't be offensive, Sun Yen," cautioned his wife.

"I knew who they were the minute they sat down. Sure, they're the Paces, own and operate Odd Jobs, Inc. They're continually getting into—"

"Jake!" warned Hildy, darting, long bare legs flashing, out of her chair. "In the aisle to your right."

There he was. Face feverish, eyes sunk in shadowy hollows and blazing. Right arm made of rusty steel, swinging up now to point directly at Jake. "Kill them both," he was chanting, "kill them both."

"Not quite yet." Grabbing up the empty chair in front of him, Jake hurled it smack into the killer.

The metal chair took the man in the chin, forcing his head far back and jerking him off his feet. As he tottered back across the aisle his hand went off and a sizzling line of red-yellow flame cut straight up through the afternoon.

"I knew we'd get ourselves killed sitting in the vicinity of those daredevils."

"Stop bitching, Sun Yen, and hit the deck."

Chairs were clacking, falling down. People were scrambling, tumbling, running, jumping, anxious to get away from there before the built-in flame gun went off again.

Jake nudged his way through the confusion, caught hold of the still-stumbling man by his gun arm. The thing was so hot it made him grit his teeth, but he twisted the arm behind the assassin's back and yanked him upright. "Who the hell are you?"

"Snuff yourself." The man ran away.

Jake realized, in under three seconds, that the guy had a way to detach the arm swiftly. Jake held on to it for another second before dropping it to take off after the man. "He's maybe heading backstage," he called to Hildy.

She, too, was on the move. Running when she could, sailing over seated people and chairs as though they were track hurdles. Her red hair a streaming banner, she reached the front of the outdoor theater ahead of the one-armed man.

He would have galloped right into her if he hadn't suddenly sprung up onto the floating stage. "Damn bitch, ought to die."

The Great Lando had remained doubled up, holding onto himself as though he were suffering violent cramps. "Death. . . . He still carries death!"

Jake heard that and, eyes on the fugitive, realized what it meant. Instead of going after him he sprinted and tackled his wife before she could leap onto the stage. "This is the time for tucking in heads," he advised, getting one hand on her shoulder and an arm around her just below her breasts.

"But we ought—"

An enormous whomping explosion.

The floating stage stopped floating, came dropping down six feet into the airlift pit. Screams and angry shouts rolled down out of the audience.

Hildy caught her breath, gave Jake a hug, shook her head, her long red hair brushing at his bony cheek. "Should have anticipated that."

"Suicide mission, kills us and then himself. I saw him going for the trigger to the damn explosives under his tunic." Jake lifted her to her feet. "Lando's warning helped."

"Yes, he seems to have known a good deal about all this. We'd best talk to . . ." She saw it in Jake's face before she turned to look at the fallen stage.

"Too late," he said. "Lando went along with the assassin."

"Now I'll never find me blooming brooch," complained the matron.

Chapter 2

"It may be my fault," the Secretary of Show Biz said while circling the huge living room of the fortified barn which served as the offices of Odd Jobs, Inc. "Then again it may not."

Jake was sitting in a floating lucite wingchair, quietly playing Portuguese fados on a twelve string guitar while watching the tree-filled five acres of their West Redding estate. Everything was orange and gold out there in the late afternoon. Beside his right foot a factspool scanner rested on the hardwood floor. "Who knew you were flying up here from the Autumn White House in Nashville?"

"The president and no one else," answered Gunther Stool. His prominent jowls were particularly twitchy this afternoon. "At least I don't think anyone else knew."

"You arrive in Connecticut to hire us," said Hildy, "and at almost the same exact moment a suicidal flamethrower takes a crack at barbecuing us and making a public spectacle of it. Figure that for a coincidence?"

Halting, eyeing her long smooth and tan legs, Stool said, "In the light of what's been happening, no, it does not strike me as a coincidence, Hildy. Though it might be."

"This fellow who tried to do us in." Jake kicked

at the scanner. "He was last heard of, before today, in Outer Alabama where he was supposed to be locked up in an institution for the dangerously insane. His arm had been deactivated."

The Secretary of Show Biz said, "Apparently he escaped."

"Apparently," agreed Hildy. "How come the Federal Police didn't know he was running free?"

"The damn asylum didn't even know it," added Jake, "until I pixphoned them just now."

"We're dealing," said Stool, "with people who have a big budget seemingly. With a big budget, you know, almost anything can be arranged."

"Whose money is it?"

"We think, and we could be wrong but I don't feel we are, we're dealing with the Amateur Mafia again."

Jake stopped playing. "They've got money sure enough."

"I hate to see them prosper," said Hildy. "I mean besides being crooks, they're such awful bigots. Not allowing any Italians into their Mafia."

"They think the Mafia is too good an idea to be wasted on European minorities," said Secretary Stool. "They've been very successful, got a net worth in the neighborhood of 2.6 billion."

"Poor Italian Mafia doesn't take in more than 20 million a year anymore," said Hildy.

Jake leaned the guitar against a half-size statue of a horse he'd recently carved from real marble. "Is the AM making another try to take over the entertainment industry?"

"Yes," answered Stool. "Or so we strongly suspect. That would account for the murders, wouldn't it?"

Hildy wandered by Jake's chair, rubbed her fingertips across the back of his neck before moving on. "Your people, Gunther, suspect these recent murders among show business figures are linked? Been five of them this year."

"Six," corrected Jake.

She gathered up the big guitar, perched on a stool and began to play an early 20th century walking-bass blues. "You insist on including Bubbles the Clown."

"That sure wasn't a suicide," Jake told his wife.

The Secretary of Show Biz scratched at his scalloped chin. "If we include Bubbles the Clown, which my department is inclined to do, the total today is seven murders."

"Seven?" echoed both Paces. Hildy ceased playing.

"This hasn't been released to the media as yet," said Stool. "Raffles Tunny was found dead, murdered, early this morning at his therapeutic chalet in Switzerland."

"Too bad," said Jake. "He was a pretty good juggler."

"How?" asked Hildy.

"What means was used to dispatch Raffles? He was stunned to death, but not by any mechanical weapon we can detect traces of."

"Ha!" Jake, bouncing in his chair, snapped his fingers. "Now I see why the president of the United States sent you to bring us into this thing, Gunther. But it sounds impossible."

"That's your specialty, isn't it? You and Hildy, as Odd Jobs, Inc. you specialize in impossible crimes and intrigues."

"Improbable," amended Hildy. "What the heck are you getting at, Jake?"

"I'll bet the pattern of the murder of Raffles

Tunny matches that of a killer named Shocker Fulson," he replied. "The guy with the electric touch."

"Shocker's dead," said Hildy. "That was a side effect of our investigation of the telekinetic pilfering down in Disneystate last spring."

Jake's eyes closed, he tilted back in his chair. "Two show-business murders back they found Rance Keane, the top gunfighter in America, dead in the middle of a bare field. No footprints around but his, yet he'd been strangled. That reminded me of Pox Fairfield, the telekinetic murderer."

"He's dead, too."

"They all are," said Stool. "Which is why, finally, the Federal Police are allowing us to contact a private inquiry agency such as yours."

"All?" Hildy, hands on hips, stopped near the easel which held the self-portrait she'd been working on earlier in the week. "You're telling us, Gunther, that the MO's on all these murders of entertainment notables match those of dead men?"

"Exactly, Hildy. Almost down to every detail, amazingly close." Stool gave an exasperated sigh. "When the Federal Police ran the details of the Raffles Tunny murder through their crime computers only one name came out as fitting the pattern used. The name was that of Shocker Fulson. There aren't, after all, that many wild talent killers in this world of ours."

"You suspect somebody, the Amateur Mafia say, is reviving the dead?"

"We've given up attempting to come up with answers, Jake. But personally I believe the Amateur Mafia has put together a gang of wild talent murderers and let them loose to plague us, a sort of death patrol."

"If they want to take over a piece of the government-controlled show business, Gunther," put in Hildy, "why are they knocking off valuable entertainers?"

"To put pressure on us. You must realize the AM is a very practical businesslike organization."

"They figure they can always find another juggler or clown," said Jake. "You have to be willing to kill a few important people if you're going to scare the U.S. government."

"They haven't made a direct pitch yet?"

"No, Hildy, nobody has openly asked for a piece of the business. They never will. Hints, however, have been popping up. Eventually someone will hint that if we don't share show business with them the killings won't stop."

Hildy went over, rubbed at Jake's neck once again. "Shocker Fulson absolutely is dead, isn't he?"

"Dead, cremated and resting in an urn down in New Orleans."

"Well, then he couldn't have murdered anyone in Switzerland this morning."

Narrowing an eye, Jake nodded at Gunther Stool. "How much are you going to pay us to find out if Shocker did or didn't?"

"$200,000."

"$200,000?" Jake shook his head. "With the risk of assassination hanging over us? The Amateur Mafia obviously doesn't want Odd Jobs, Inc. digging into this."

"The president's been very touchy about budgets of late, Jake. After the Secretary of War dipped into the bribe fund and then Mrs. Hobart ordered all those $3 bills printed up we—"

CALLING DR. PATCHWORK 15

"How high did they tell you to go to get us, Gunther?" Hildy asked him.

"Well, $400,000."

Her green eyes blinked at her husband. "Shall we?"

"Since it's a favor for the government I guess we can work for a fee that low," he decided. "Half in front, Gunther."

"Oh, no. Best I can do, Jake, is $50,000 now, then $150,000 when you solve the case and the final $200,000 when the next fiscal—"

"Whoa," advised Jake. "You don't understand the deal. We get $400,000 whether we catch anybody or not. Our fees aren't based on any kind of guaranteed results."

"I don't know if I can swing that."

Hildy moistened her upper lip with her tongue. "We've been 87 percent successful in the past year."

"89 percent," said Jake.

"Oh, you keep including the Baroness Honeyball Job, Jake, which got solved only because she happened to think your game of tennis was—"

"I tracked her down, damn it, Hildy. Tennis had very little to do with—"

"We're desperate," said the Secretary of Show Biz. "The president is deathly afraid they may even strike at Fancy Dawntreader, robbing him of his favorite vidshow."

"Who?" said Hildy.

"Fancy Dawntreader, the gossip," said Jake. "Very attractive young woman if you like tallness."

"I'm tall."

"She's six feet seven."

"That is tall."

"Has someone threatened her?"

"No." The flesh on Stool's heavy face jiggled. "They never give us a warning, though, they simply strike. Bam! Like that and another valuable show-business personality is lost forever."

Jake stood, took another look at the waning day outside. "Stick $150,000 in our Banx account, Gunther, and hand us the rest in cash for expenses."

After several long seconds Gunther Stool said, "Very well, you've got a deal."

"I'll fly down to New Orleans and see what really happened to Shocker," said Jake. "Hildy, you check out the Raffles Tunny murder site."

"Fine," said his wife, smiling, "I always like Switzerland."

Stool said, "The Federal Police and the International Lawforce have already done both those things."

Jake grinned a thin grin. "Even so," he said.

Chapter 3

———————

Jake leaned back in his synwicker chair, gazed up at the seethrough bulletproof dome ceiling of their dining room. The night sky was incredibly clear, rich with stars. "Too much bay leaf," he said, wiping at his lips with a neolin napkin. "Yeah, a touch too much."

Hildy made a polite snorting sound. "A lot you know about preparing Coquilles St. Jacques."

"Didn't I win a blue ribbon for cooking this very dish?"

A louder snort. "At the Nebraska State Fair." She took up the bottle of white wine to refill her glass.

"You still need to learn how to take criticism, Hildy." Jake pushed back from the floating oval table, walked to the cobbler's bench on which he'd earlier dumped a batch of factspools and a small stack of faxgrams.

"It was your turn to cook anyway." Rim of her wine glass touching her chin, she watched her lanky husband.

"Going to have to dig out that ribbon. I'm fairly certain it was won in Paris."

"The farmer who pinned it on you was wearing a French cologne." She stretched up out of her chair. "Back to work?"

Squatting, Jake was setting the nine spools out in a single row. "You'll be leaving for Switzerland early in the morning, and I'll be catching a Trans-Am flight to New Orleans. I want us to know all about these show business murders before we depart," he said, riffling the faxgrams. "Got coded responses from six of our stringers so far, with some background stuff neither the Feds or IntLaw have. There'll be more when Steranko the Siphoner sends us what he can hijack from the Amateur Mafia's clandestine computers."

Hildy crossed over to stand behind him. Her slender fingers rubbed at the back of his neck. "Certain you want us to take this case?"

"I like the fee." He stood to face her, put his hands on her bare shoulders.

"The people who want to stop us, be they Amateur Mafia or whoever, have been pretty darn ruthless already," Hildy said. "This afternoon's assassin could have killed a lot more people besides the Great Lando, including us."

"That's one of the things Odd Jobs, Inc. does, remember?" He kissed her. "We take risks."

Arms around him, Hildy said, "Okay, I won't mention it again. After all, I'm as do-or-die as you. Sorry if I had a moment when I felt I didn't want to see you end up like that poor magician today."

Jake cleared his throat. "We don't have to scan this material immediately."

"No, that's true." Her fingertips moved around to the front sealseam of his shirt.

Up under the skydome an orange light blossomed. Jake noticed it first. "Emergency phone," he said.

With a resigned shrug Hildy let go of him to go walking in long-legged strides to the pixphone alcove. After flicking the response button on the orange phone, she said, "Odd Jobs, Inc. We never sleep."

"Doggone if you ain't prettier than the last time I seen you, Hildy. And you was already cuter than a bug's fanny even then."

"So my entomologist friends keep telling me. How are you, Mr. President?"

A chunky blond man in a white cowboy suit and Stetson showed on the plate-size phone screen. "Aw, jist call me Ramblin' Billy. I don't cotton to no high-falutin' talk when I'm a-jawin' with my old buddies. Is your man to home?"

"Stand by, Ramblin' Billy." With a crooked smile on her face, Hildy motioned to Jake.

"Evening, Ramblin' Billy," Jake said when he was in the alcove and being picked up by the sending camera. "You still in Nashville?"

"Havin' me a hotdog of a time, too," said the President of the United States. "Got my old lady with me, and my brother Hicky . . . You remember Hicky, don't you, used to play electric violin in my group 'fore I become president?"

"A gifted fellow."

"Ain't he, though," agreed Ramblin' Billy Dahlman, chuckling. "Also got Cousin Lanolin here and Granpappy Rooster and Cousin Sawny Bean. Havin' us a hotdog of a time."

"Has Secretary Stool reported to you?"

"That's why I got on this dingus to you, Jake," said the president. "I'm dang happy you and your missus agreed to tackle this here caper. Makes me mighty happy. Remember when I made my hit record, *Feels Like A Warm Puppy Dog's A-Slurpin' At My Heart?* Wellsir, that's how this here ol' president feels about you helpin' out."

"Haven't done much yet," Jake said. "We're just getting down to studying the—"

"Aw, just knowin' you two's thinkin' about it makes me feel good all over." President Dahlman glanced to his left. "Cousin Biddy, you can't do that to a parrot. Got no sense that girl. Third bird she wrecked this trip. Stop, you hear, Biddy." When he returned his attention to Jake his pudgy face was serious, voice lower. "Couple small things I want to pass along to you folks."

"Pass," invited Jake.

"I done had a hit eight, nine years back, a platinum hit. Name of it were *Ever Time My Hair Stands Up My Baby Do Me Wrong.* I want to tell you, Jake, and Hildy, too, I got me one of them hair standin' and flesh a-crawlin' moods upon me right now for sure." He twisted off his white hat to fan his suddenly perspiring face. "Got me a premonition that they's going to kill Fancy Dawntreader. An' I surely am fond of that gal."

"We'll see she isn't killed, Ramblin' Billy," Jake promised. "If it turns out she's in any danger at all."

"Boy, oh boy." Fanning himself again, the President of the United States chuckled, though with some nervousness. "Here I can handle all kinds of big national and international problems and I go an' let a few little murders get to me. Must be my country boy instincts a-workin'. Cousin Jeddy, you oughtn't to do that right on the rug. You stop that now, boy."

"Was there anything else?" inquired Jake.

Ramblin' Billy pulled his Stetson back on, swallowed, tried to smile. "Don't get mad now," he said as a sheepish look touched his broad face. "You probably heard tell I'm havin' me a bit of trouble controlling the Federal Police these days. Well, shucks . . . thing is, Jake, I simply can't stop 'em from puttin' a special agent of their own on this to sort of keep tabs on you."

Hildy poked Jake in the small of the back. "Who? It better not be who I think it's going to be."

"We don't want the FP butting in," Jake told the president. "In fact, when you come to Odd Jobs, Inc. and pay my fees you—"

"Don't suppose you could lop 25 thou of them fees, by the way, Jake?"

"No."

"Don't think so. Ain't me who's poor-mouthin', it's the dang Congress."

"Who?" repeated Hildy, with another poke.

"Who's FP putting on this?"

President Dahlman said, "Now I know he's got a reputation for bein' sort of a hellraiser, Jake, but—"

"Lars Brasher," Jake and Hildy Pace said in unison. "The Wildcat."

Ramblin' Billy nodded, avoiding the eye of his sending camera. "You got it on the first guess, folks. It's going to be Lars 'Wildcat' Brasher and . . . what's that, Cousin Pridey? Oh, listen, Jake, I got to go. Fancy Dawntreader's about due on the TV. Good luck, you hear?"

Before Jake finished saying, "Thanks," the pixphone screen was black.

"Wildcat." Hildy spun on one foot, headed to the dinner table to retrieve her glass of wine.

"I'll talk to Gunther Stool, have that—"

"Come on, Jake. If the gosh darn president can't call Wildcat off, Gunther sure as hell can't."

"Probably not, you're right."

After a sip of wine, Hildy said, "Wildcat nearly screwed us up good in Stand Oil Arabia Christmas before last when we were working on that invisible man business. Barging into that Exxon harem with two blaster pistols going. No finesse."

Jake returned to his scatter of factspools. "He probably still has a grudge against me."

"I imagine so, after you broke his arm in Tangiers during Easter vacation."

"Only sprained it."

"I heard the bones cracking."

"Wildcat was probably thinking at that particular moment. His skull always makes those funny rusty sounds when he tries to think."

"Wildcat." Hildy drained her glass, filled it once more. "Jake, is Ramblin' Billy a good president?"

"Better than that Democrat-Republican nitwit we had in there," her husband answered. "I feel more comfortable with the Republican-Democrat party back in power. Besides which, it's refreshing hearing *Hail To The Chief* played Country & Western style."

"I suppose I should have confidence in somebody who wears a white cowboy hat, and yet . . ." She shrugged her lovely shoulders.

Jake slotted a factspool into a scanner, slumped into a lycra slingchair. Facts and images unfolded on the small scanner screen. As he watched Jake made an occasional mumbling noise.

Hildy decided to set her latest glass of wine back on the table untasted. Hands behind her back, she stared up at the night sky. "Jake, if I told you I had one of those downhome hunches, the kind Ramblin' Billy gets, would you trust it?"

"Huh? Din't quite catch what you—"

"Nothing, never mind." She made her way to the cobbler's bench, selected a factspool and a scanner of her own. Inches away from sitting in a floating streetchair, she rose again. "I'm going to watch her, too."

"Who?"

Hildy turned on a ball-shape floating TV set which hovered to the left of the dining-room table. "The prez' favorite, Fancy Dawntreader."

". . . for Fancy's Focus, the show-business gossip show viewed by more people than any similar show on television. Yes, Fancy's Focus which stars the most beautiful, and the tallest, scandalmonger in the western world. Now direct from her magnificent home in New Beverly Hills, here is . . . Fancy Dawntreader."

"Wow," murmured Hildy.

The television screen showed her a very lacy boudoir. Reclining on a wide circular and pink-sheeted bed was a long tan girl with hair the color of falling snow. She was stunning. If she hadn't talked through her nose, the languid, seductive image would have been overwhelming.

"Hi ya," greeted Fancy Dawntreader, absently stroking the considerable portion of her left thigh which showed through her filmy black nightdress. "Got all kindsa dirt for ya, show-biz fans . . ."

"She shouldn't chew bubble gum," said Hildy. "That definitely detracts."

"It's not gum," said Jake, looking up from his scanner. "It's a plastic tranquilizer."

"How do you know?"

"I keep up with show business."

Hildy pulled the stretchair over to sit in.

". . . tonight Fancy Dawntreader is sending," the lengthy and beautiful girl was saying, "a big bouquet of red, red roses to Sentimental Sid, whose electronic ballads are packing 'em in up there in Frisco. They said Sid was washed up, but I'm here to tell ya he's climbing right back to the top. And Sid, although nearly twenny-eight, will have a golden hit any day now. Remember, folks, I never dropped Sentimental Sid, even when he was on the skids and was seen rolling in gutters and poorly paved streets in Black Oakland, a dopey-eyed slave to plastic tranquilizers . . ."

"Good for Sid," remarked Hildy.

"Are you," asked her husband, "going to monitor the whole and entire broadcast?"

"I am, yes. I feel it's my duty to keep up with show business."

". . . this'll make ya cry, folks. It did me, an you know Fancy Dawntreader is one tough bimbo. Anyways, I jist got word one of the greats of the vaudeville world is no more. Yeah, the late great Raffles Tunny is a goner. Give a look at this film clip of Raffles, taken in better days when the poor simp was still alive and kicking . . ."

"How's she know about Raffles?" said Hildy. "Gunther told us they weren't releasing the news until tomorrow."

"Fancy Dawntreader has sources, same as we do," said Jake as he put his scanner aside. "There's something else," he muttered, getting up.

"Beg pardon?"

He walked a wide circle around his abandoned chair. "Can't get it, but it's something about Fancy Dawntreader and Raffles Tunny," he said, frowning. "Eludes me."

"Important?"

"Possibly yes, possibly no." Seating himself, he returned his attention to the factspool.

"We're all gonna miss ya, Raffles," said Fancy Dawntreader out in Southern California.

Chapter 4

———◆———

"That's not the way to mix a Bearded Lady," Jake told the girl bartender.

"It isn't?" The exquisite blonde behind the skyliner luxury class bar blushed affectingly.

"A Bearded Lady is two pinches of *kelp*, a jigger of white rum and a splash of mineral water," he explained. "Not two pinches of freeze-dried anise."

The blush deepened before it faded away. "I told them down at the Equal Employment Office I'm not cut out for this job," the incredibly beautiful bartender confided across the floating pseudo-ivory bar top. "Not suited at all. I mean it isn't merely my fear of heights, though lord knows hurtling through the sky in a gigantic jet doesn't help that. No, it's rather the fact I'm a true scatterbrain, can't keep all these drink recipes straight in my head. And this stupid TransAm insists we can't use premixes."

"Let's hope so."

"Well, see? You're obviously a man with an educated palate. Me, I've a dumbunny palate. Booze is booze to me, all tastes alike." She rested her delicate elbows on the fake ivory, dropped her voice to a more confiding tone. "Would you believe a few minutes ago I couldn't even remember how to mix a Martini. Nearly scared that trio of Japanese

26

business men over there to death by dropping cherries in theirs." She shook her head in mock despair.

Jake moved the base of his ineptly mixed Bearded Lady's glass a fraction of an inch to the right. "You can console yourself with the fact you have excellent taste in perfume," he said, smiling directly at her.

The fantastically beautiful girl blushed again. "I'm not wearing perfume."

Scratching at the side of his nose, Jake gave the girl one of his bony grins. "How are you supposed to account for that faint plastic scent you give off? It's a definite flaw, one I've run up against before." Very casually Jake left his stool at the otherwise unoccupied bar counter.

The incredibly beautiful girl dipped her blonde head once in the direction of the three Japanese business men who sat around a nearby table with bright red cherries in their Martinis. Giving up their skywindow view of the cloud formations between Manhattan and New Orleans, they rose as one.

"A moment of your time, Occidental sir?" requested the smallest of the three bizsuited Japanese men.

Jake sniffed. "You guys, too?" He rubbed his hand across the back of his neck. When he'd begun to realize what the lady bartender was he'd deftly transferred a palmsize disabler to his traveltunic collar. When his hand left his neck the disabler rod rested, unobtrusively, in his palm. "Your bosses apparently don't know all brand-new androids give off a slight but detectable new android smell."

"It is impolite to mention a fellow person's body odors, Occidental, sir."

"Manufactured by Kål-Hjerne Industries in Denmark, I'd guess, going by the smell and the texture of your synskin." Slowly and carefully Jake was backing toward the circular stairway which would take him back up to his passenger floor in the giant skyliner. "What have they programmed you all to do? Another simple assassination try?"

"This man is in my way," complained a small unhappy voice behind Jake. "The man's in the way. I can't get in to have the Pepsi on the rocks you promised me, Gram. The man's in the way. Everything's spoiled."

"Hush, hush, Byron. All you need do is ask the nice-looking young man to step aside."

A quick glance showed Jake a little boy in a strained two-piece funsuit accompanied by a plump grey-haired woman. They were standing at the foot of the circular staircase and had to pass around Jake to get into the cocktail lounge.

"He's never going to move, Gram. He's going to stand and stand here forever. I'm never going to get my two Pepsis." He waved a miniature pistol angrily.

"One, Byron. Grammy only promised you one Pepsi."

"No, you . . . *Bong!*"

Jake had, unexpectedly, spun and dived. He poked the tip of the disabling device against the base of the little boy's skull.

Being an android, the little boy could do nothing else but become disabled and cease to function. He would remain in that state for several hours. All Kål-Hjerne androids had an Achilles spot at the skull-spine connecting point.

Giving the plump grandmother a jab of the disabler as he climbed by her, Jake went galloping up the twisting steps. "Six andies," he was saying to himself. "They must have some budget."

"Sir, has TransAm Airways done something to offend you?" At the top of the stairs a breathtakingly beautiful Negro stewardess awaited him. She had one hand behind her back.

Not even pausing to sniff, Jake smacked her with his disabler.

"Surely, sir, you . . . *spong!*"

"Seven." Jake edged around her, moved down the short corridor which led to the luxury-class seating section of the aircraft. Halting inches from the neoglass beaded curtain at the corridor's end, he took several deep breaths in through his nose. "You've been nodding at the switch, Jake old boy," he chided himself.

The smell, usually imperceptible to untrained nostrils, of new androids came clearly to him now. He'd sat in this section for almost a half hour before descending to the cocktail lounge and he hadn't tumbled to the fact all his fellow passengers were andies.

Putting his eye to a break between curtain and wall he counted the house. "Fifteen, plus the piano player. Christ, their budget's got to be even bigger than ours."

The luxury class section was built to resemble a ski lodge of the last century. Comfortable leather and rough wood chairs, a huge, highly believable fireplace and an upright piano with a gold-toothed Negro playing rags upon it.

"The rest of the andies from the cocktail lounge didn't follow me," he reflected. "So maybe these aren't set to do me in either. It's a shade puzzling."

He backed off, silently ran back down the corridor. From a side pocket of his travelsuit he took

another small tool. Clutching it and the disabler together, he went up the stairway to the top floor of
the skyliner.

"This, sir, isn't the time for passengers, even our
pampered and petted luxury class passengers, to be
up here where our skilled pilots are at work." A
large, wide steward met him in the corridor leading
to the pilot suite.

"Looks like I got my signals crossed, doesn't it."
Jake scratched his head, swung his arm down to
give the android a shot of the disabling rod.

The pilot suite held three people. The navigator,
seated behind a wingshape desk. The pilot, a mid-
dlesize man who was slouched in the driveseat idly
watching the robot control board. The co-pilot, a
handsome Chinese girl seemingly asleep in a
relaxchair.

"Off limits, sir," said the navigator in a Southern
drawl.

"Dialects even," said Jake. "That's even more expensive, particularly with the way Kål-Hjerne
hikes their prices for little extras like that.

"Hold off now, cracker, what you . . . *Bung!*"

"TransAm ships are swipe-proof, if that's the
kind of . . . *Bong!*"

"What the hell?" The Chinese girl sat up. "You
can't . . . *Bing!*"

Jake nudged the disabled andy pilot out of his
seat. "Light-weight models, too. Very impressive."
He took the pilot's place, scanning the control
panel. "We're not heading for New Orleans at all.
If I'm reading these things correctly, our destina-
tion is . . . yep, an island in the Caribbean. Probably San Norberto."

He rocked in the chair a few times. Then
reached down to attach a small silver disc the size

of a Swedish pancake to the forehead of the pilot android.

The mechanism groaned, opening his eyes. "I am at your service, most illustrious master. Though I know not what devilish device you have placed against my authentic and believable skonce, yet in my heart of hearts I am compelled—"

"Yeah, okay," Jake interrupted. "You've got a simple parasite control running you now, a variation on the common ones that I designed myself."

"Ah, your skill is indeed marvelous, grand sir. The mind of this humble servant is awed at the mere—"

"Whose idea is all this?"

"As much as I burn, oh master mine, to answer you truthfully, yet I fearfully must admit I do not understand your question."

"We're in a damn good imitation of a TransAm jet," Jake told the fallen mechanism. "Somebody arranged to substitute it at Manhattan Airport 3. They rerouted all the other passengers except me. They staffed it and peopled it with what has to be a hundred plus very expensive androids. I want to know why?"

"It is because, sire, someone wishes to talk to you. Someone to whom the opportunity to ingest the brilliant words which fall from your magnificent tongue is worth any and all expense. Nay, it—"

"What's the guy's name?"

"Bobby Thatcher."

Jake nodded. "The head of the Amateur Mafia."

"You have said it, master."

Jake detached the parasite, the android sank back to his completely disabled state on the suite floor.

"Well, if the head of the Amateur Mafia wants to talk to me, I may as well go to see him."

After making sure the robot flying equipment was functioning properly, Jake went over and dumped the Chinese girl co-pilot off her chair. He took her place.

The rest of the flight was uneventful.

Chapter 5

Hildy set aside the violin and stepped off the bandstand to see about retrieving her clothes.

"Ah, Fraulein Einfuhr, you were superlative." A small dark-haired man had come running across the darkening sound stage to catch Hildy by the naked elbow.

"Thank you, Herr Scherz." Hildy, besides being totally unclothed, had braided light blonde hair now and was calling herself Irma Einfuhr. She spoke flawless German.

"To come to our aid at the last moment, after we learned poor Ursula had sprained an ankle." Scherz shook his head, absently patting Hildy on her bare buttocks. "How could a girl as agile as Ursula sprain an ankle, it's a puzzler."

"A puzzler truly."

"Put this on, put this on. The show is over." A thickset woman came out of the wings to hand Hildy a flowered robe.

Glancing back at the other girls who made up the nudist string quartet, Hildy let the wardrobe mistress help her into the neosilk robe. "It must have been, as you so sweetly pointed out earlier, Herr Scherz, fate itself which prompted me to show up here today to ask for a part on *Naked Shadows*."

"Fate it was, my dear Irma, a most kind fate,"

agreed Scherz. "It is far from easy, I can assure you, to cast the only nudist soap opera on Swiss television. You see them with their clothes on, they look fine. But nude, ah, it's a very different story. Take Weber over there, a brilliant actor but, frankly, we receive many complaints about those blotches on his backside. You noticed them?"

"When he danced through my scene, yes."

"He dances well enough I suppose, for a man so corpulent," Scherz continued. "It is important with a nudist soap opera that one's flesh doesn't jiggle too much when one is dancing." He smiled up at the blonde Hildy. "Allow me to compliment you on your lack of jiggling, Irma."

"One doesn't jiggle much playing Mozart," she told him. "Now, if you will excuse me, I must get to the dressing room before I take a chill."

"Yes, yes, to be sure. We can't have such a brilliant new addition to our cast coming down with the grippe." The director escorted her across the television studio and down the dim corridor leading to the lesser players' dressing room. "When once again you have clothed your admirable body, Irma, perhaps we can enjoy a cup of cocoa next door at the Zahnburste Rosa. There is much to talk about, including a possible contract for you."

"I fear I promised another of the young ladies in the quartet to take coffee with her, Herr Scherz," Hildy told him as she reached for the door knob. "However, I will be free at the dinner hour."

The small director brightened. "Then by all means let us have dinner. Where and when may I call for you?"

"Number 77 Heinzwackstrasse," improvised Hildy.

"A very pleasant neighborhood."

"I find it so. Until seven this evening then." She went into the dressing room.

"Don't let him talk you into any extra rehearsals," advised the blonde girl at the dressing table next to Hildy's.

"He doesn't seem too formidable, Greta."

Greta Kedeling sighed. "Perhaps he isn't," she said, studying her pretty face in the bluish makeup mirror. "I suppose the real problem is I'm too gullible. I believe everyone."

"That can be a handicap." Hildy fetched her clothes out of the wardrobe cabinet assigned to her a few hours earlier.

"It was the same way when I worked for you-know-who." The half-dressed girl did a bit of pantomime juggling. "Many were the times he talked me into taking off my clothes, and he wasn't even a nudist soap opera director."

"We can talk about it at coffee," suggested Hildy with a friendly smile.

Their waiter was a highly polished chrome robot of vaguely humanoid style. He was filigreed profusely and the music box built into his chest broke into lullabies at odd moments. "Two hot chocolates and two napoleons. Yum. yum. That sounds good."

From their carved-wood booth in the cozy coffee house there was a view of the slanting cobbled street outside, tile rooftops, spotless white and pink buildings and, far off, a ridge of snowy mountain tops. The late afternoon sky was a barely polluted blue.

"You're a very easy person to talk to," said Greta as their waiter rolled away over the hardwood plank floor.

"Try to be," said Hildy.

"You know, I never confided in poor Ursula," admitted the girl. "Yet we played side by side in the *Naked Shadows* quartet for over six months. Do the show every day, then rush back to Raffles Tunny's chalet to be his housemaid, as he euphemistically called it. Sometimes I wonder if show business is really worth it."

"What are you going to do now Raffles Tunny's gone?"

"I really don't know, Irma. Herr Scherz claims he can get me into a cabaret act, and I'd only have to be semi-nude in that. Somehow, though, I don't quite trust him."

"Yum yum." Their waiter was back with two steaming mugs of chocolate and two pastries. His metal thumb had penetrated one of the napoleons and he licked filling off it while rolling away.

"I shouldn't eat all this sort of stuff," said Greta with a downward frown at her napoleon. "You may not have noticed, but I'm developing a little roll of fat right around here." She drew a line around her slim waist.

"With all you've been through, I'd think you'd be losing weight."

"Not me. The more grief they pile on me, the more I chomp. When my mother died I gained six pounds. Seeing poor Raffles get shocked to death I . . . oops!" She pressed her fingertips to her lips, lowering her head. "No one is supposed to know I was a witness to that."

No one did, Hildy had found out during her first hour here in Gewüfznecke, Switzerland. Both the local police and the International Lawforce agent who covered this canton suspected Greta knew somewhat more than she was admitting, but had nothing concrete. Since the Geneva Crime Accords of 1999 the use of any kind of truth-eliciting drugs or devices was forbidden except in the case of a threat to national security. No one could figure how to stretch the stun murder of a vaudeville juggler into a threat to the safety of Switzerland, so what Greta knew remained her secret.

Odd Jobs, Inc. however, had an informant in this part of the country and he possessed a touch of psi powers. Enough to have a firm hunch Raffles' housemaid had actually witnessed the killing. The informant had also been able to help Hildy locate another member of the *Naked Shadows* music group and bribe her into feigning an ankle sprain.

"It must have been terrible," said Hildy, placing a hand over the girl's.

"I thought he was going to do it to me. I really did. And do you know what my first reaction was? I got terribly hungry."

Hildy said, "He left you alone, though, the killer."

"Just like, almost, I wasn't there," Greta said. "He must have seen me, since I was in the bedroom doorway. See, Raffles was having a 'bot massage in his room and I was freshening up in my room and I heard this . . . oh, it was an awful sound. As though Raffles had picked up something unexpectedly hot. He howled with pain and surprise. He gave this one awful scream, which is what made me come running. There's another thing about me, Irma, I always seem to run toward trouble."

"Didn't the man see you at all?"

"I can't be sure. He turned his face toward me . . . but . . ." The slim girl began to tremble. "He didn't have much of a face." She passed her palm across her own face. "He had eyes, little mean sort of eyes and very strange white eyebrows. But from the eyes down there wasn't anything. No nose, no mouth."

"Faceless Slim!" exclaimed Hildy. "But he's dead, too."

"What?"

"Nothing, Greta. Your description reminded me of someone I used to know."

Another shudder. "Who'd want to know such an awful-looking person."

"Didn't he aim his weapon at you?"

"Weapon?"

"The thing he used to kill Raffles."

"There wasn't any gun or anything." Greta shook her head. "I'm absolutely certain. Everything about that scene, it's inside my head. I don't even want it, but there it is. The faceless man did not have a weapon. When I reached the threshold he was still touching Raffles. He had his hand on poor Raffles' arm, right about here." She seemed to get a shock when she touched her upper arm. "Then he let go and Raffles just rolled off the table and his body was all stiff and his poor wispy hair was standing straight up and he hit the floor with a terrible hard smack and the sunlight made stripes across his naked back."

Hildy went around to the girl's side of the booth. She put an arm around her shoulders. "Okay, that's enough. You don't have to talk about it any more now."

"I never have, until today," said Greta. "I didn't tell the police because I just wanted to get away from there. Being a witness to a murder, having to try to identify people and swearing to things. I'd gain a hundred pounds under all that pressure. So I didn't actually lie, I simply didn't tell them quite everything." She turned her head toward Hildy.

"You won't tell?"

"No."

Fifteen minutes later the two women left the coffee house. Their robot waiter followed them to the door, spewing good wishes and lullabies. They parted at the first corner and Hildy went walking back toward her hotel.

"Killed Raffles with Shocker Fulson's MO, except he looks like Faceless Slim," she was thinking. "What kind of clues are these? These only lead us to a pair of dead men. And all the stuff Jake and I went through last night seems to indicate the other killings were done by more dead criminals. Is Gunther right about the AM setting up a nonsched resurrection business to . . ."

Hildy sensed something dropping down on her from above.

Too late to stop a heavy body from hitting her, a powerful arm from circling her throat. Too late to stop the needle from jabbing into her skin.

Too late.

Chapter 6

———◆———

Three strides from the bottom of the disembark ramp Jake unexpectedly executed a somersault. He hit the twilight landing field flat-footed and with a blaster pistol in his right hand. "No guns necessary," he said.

The big man who'd been awaiting him at the foot of the imitation TransAm's ramp was surprised to find the tip of Jake's gun touching his neck. "They're merely a precaution, sir."

"Not essential. Get rid of them."

"As you say." The big Amateur Mafia lieutenant dropped his stungun.

"No guns at all," said Jake. "This is a sociable call."

The other five AM greeters scowled, shifted their big feet, mumbled. Then they let their weapons fall. Puffs of dust spritzed up into the waning day.

"How many of our androids did you wreck?" the big man asked as Jake lowered the blaster some.

"Disabled around a dozen, including two just now getting down here from the pilot suite." Jake grinned a bleak grin at the watching AM members and at the dry treeless stretch of San Norberto Island he'd landed on. "No permanent damage done,

trust me. You really don't need such high price andies."

"The Amateur Mafia, unlike some dago outfits
with similar names, always goes first class," the big
man informed him. "I must admit that when we realized you'd taken over our aircraft, we were con-
cerned. Mrs. Thatcher especially was fearful. She
keeps a stern eye on expenses."

"Thatcher's mother is here on the island with
him?"

"Would he move his headquarters from Brazil
and not bring his mother?"

"Why the move anyway?"

"Oh, when those dumb Portugees actually held
an election and dumped the dictator . . . Bobby
Thatcher saw the handwriting on the wall. Brazil's
no safer than America now."

Jake said, "Thatcher wants to talk to me."

"That was the purpose of this elaborate strata-
gem, yes."

"You could have arranged an interview a lot
cheaper."

"Exactly what Mrs. Thatcher pointed out. I'll escort you to the game preserve now." The lieutenant reached for Jake's arm, thought better of it
and allowed his hand to drop to his side. "Bobby
would like you to join in a bit of hunting while
you have your talk."

"I don't kill for sport."

"Our preserve is stocked exclusively with robot
animals." He gestured at a large fenced-in area a
quarter of a mile away. "This way, please."

Jake walked side by side with the man. The others remained behind, muttering but making no im-
mediate effort to pick up their discarded weapons.

". . . a leopard's a leopard. Why do you need

two of them, Bobby?" someone was inquiring in a high creaky voice on the other side of the bamboo game preserve fence.

"This one's a panther, Mom. Not the same thing."

"This bill has got to be a mistake. Am I right? From Fildix, Ltd. for one simulacra panther . . . it still looks a hell of a lot like the leopard to me . . . for one simulacra panther, $100,000. You could buy yourself a real panther and a couple nice girls besides for that kind of money."

"Mom, it's a very reasonable price for a robot black panther. We got a special organized crime discount from Fildix, otherwise it would have—"

"So how come three elephants? You going to tell me one of them is a panther, too, and my failing old eyes are misleading me?"

"We'll send one back, Mom. Okay?"

"One?"

"You've got to have two elephants at least, Mom, or big game hunting is no fun," Bobby Thatcher explained. "Look, I'm the head of the biggest crime syndicate ever known. You want people to think when I go big game hunting all I got is one elephant?"

"You really like all three of them, Bobby?"

"You know I do, Mom."

"Okay, okay, I'm a softy. You can keep them."

Jake's guide knocked discreetly on the fence gate. It produced a dry rattling sound. "Mr. Thatcher, your guest is here."

"Guest?" came Mrs. Thatcher's voice. "There's a big laugh. He wrecks about $500,000 worth of expensive robots and—"

"Androids, Mom. And they're not actually ruined, only—"

"Come in, come in, Mr. Robot Smasher." The gate was yanked open by a plump woman in a two-piece funsuit of a sunburst pattern. "Maybe you can wreck our $240,000 elephant while you're here."

Bobby Thatcher was a tall freckled man with sandy hair. He held an electronic game rifle under one arm. "Welcome to my island, Mr. Pace," he said, offering his hand. "This is my mother."

Jake shook the Amateur Mafia leader's hand while scanning the artificial jungle which stretched away from them. There were palm trees, vines, flowering shrubs, ferns covering at least three full acres. "I understand you want to talk to me," he said.

"Here's a man with a wonderful grasp of things," remarked Thatcher's mother. "We blow a ton of money to drag him here for a conference and he comes traipsing in and says, 'Could it be you want to talk to me?' "

"I'll be," Jake said to Thatcher, ignoring the plump old woman, "leaving for New Orleans in an hour. So maybe you'd better start talking."

"Busts $1,000,000 worth of the best robots money can buy," said Mrs. Thatcher, "then tells us when he's coming and going."

"I'll leave you now, Mr. Pace," said his escort while backing out through the gate. "Nice meeting you."

"We'll go hunting now," Thatcher told Jake.

"I'm not much interested in—"

"Mom hates the sport. She never comes along."

"Don't let that stop you, Bobby," said his plump mother. "I'll sit here all by myself while you and Mr. Robot Buster enjoy yourselves."

Thatcher hurried across the mossy ground to a

gun rack which was attached to the bole of a tree. "Pick a rifle for yourself, Pace," he invited. "They work fine on the robot animals, but the most they can do to humans is shock them a little."

"Comforting to know." Without much deliberation Jake chose a weapon.

Thatcher led him into the twilight jungle.

"What did you want to talk about?" Jake asked.

"You're a very quick-thinking man, Pace." Thatcher was studying the shadowy jungle they were moving through. "Nothing surprises you. You realized you'd walked into a trap scant moments after you were aboard our fake TransAm. You responded swiftly to that unexpected challenge, took the initiative—"

"You sound like a blurb," interrupted Jake. "Or some kind of pitch. I'm not for hire by the AM, if that's what you're leading up to."

"More's the pity," responded Thatcher. "But I didn't arrange to have you brought here to make you a job offer."

"I don't bribe too well either. I won't drop the show business murders investigation."

"No, we didn't think you'd . . . Ah!" Thatcher swung his rifle up and squeezed the trigger.

There was a crashing sound in the underbrush, followed by three gong sounds.

"There's three hundred points for me," said Thatcher, pleased. "That's what a fatal hit on a panther earns you. I'm out in front, Pace."

"About the reason you wanted this talk?"

"Controlling a good deal more of show business in the United States would be very pleasant," said Thatcher, still watchful of the darkening jungle. "We have, I don't deny, made efforts in the past to . . ."

Jake had suddenly aimed his weapon at a patch of shadows and fired.

"Ow! Yowie!"

"How many points is that?" he asked his host.

"Afraid you've stunned one of my guards," said Thatcher. "You all right in there, Barney?"

"I'm all a-tingle, boss, all a-tingle."

"It'll pass," Thatcher assured the shadows. "Here's what I want you to understand, Pace. We're not involved in these murders."

"Is that the imperial we or do you mean . . . excuse me." Jake paused to shoot again, to his left this time.

Something in the twilight between the trees gonged five times.

"You bagged the lion," said Thatcher. "That's five hundred points. Some luck you've got, Pace."

"Are you telling me," resumed Jake, "no one in the Amateur Mafia is responsible for the killings?"

Thatcher slowed. There was a decorative fallen log beside the trail and he sat himself down on it. "I really don't think so."

"Meaning?"

"If, in the course of your investigation you find out . . . well, that there's maybe something like a splinter group forming within the Amateur Mafia, I'd appreciate your letting me know."

"I can't promise you anything," Jake said, leaning against a wide tree trunk. "Is that what you suspect?"

"As you know, we've got one of the best intelligence gathering setups in the world. Infinitely better than the Federal Police or the National Security Office up in the states," said Thatcher. "Lately, though, I . . . it's only a hunch but I have the feeling there's a schism in the works."

"And some of these splinter people are behind the show biz killings?"

"I think so, yes. Though I can't get any real evidence."

"Shocker Fulson," said Jake. "He used to work for you."

"For awhile," admitted Thatcher slowly. "Shocker's dead, you ought to know better than anyone."

"You're absolutely certain?"

Thatcher didn't answer for nearly a half minute. "Will you believe me when I tell you I'm not trying to set you up for anything?"

"Depends."

"In New Orleans, see if you can find a girl who calls herself Quebec."

"Who is she?"

"Works for us, worked for us. Well, I don't know exactly what tense to use," said the Amateur Mafia leader. "She is or was in charge of the twelve to fourteen year old division of our juve prostitution."

"Sounds like a fine person."

"She's a sweet girl, if she's still alive. Not more than eighteen herself. In fact, Quebec moved up through the ranks from one of our juvie houses down in the bayou country around—"

"I don't need a testimonial about the opportunities to strive and win while getting screwed," cut in Jake. "What's this Quebec girl got to do with the murders?"

"She pixphoned one of our New Orleans executives, fellow named Swan. Told him she'd come across something about Shocker Fulson, something odd and strange."

Night had fallen, darkness filled the imitation jungle.

"Did she disappear before she passed over what she knew?"

"Exactly. That was nearly a week ago, and we haven't been able to find her since," said Thatcher. "You know how good the AM is at rooting out people it wants to find. This girl has got to be really well hidden."

"Or dead."

"Another strong possibility, yes."

"Okay, when I get to New Orleans I'll talk to your man Swan," said Jake. "Should this turn out to be—"

"Pace, you're a very capable man." Thatcher rose up. "But I assure you I could have killed you several times over since you arrived on my island. I'm not going to go to the expense of setting an elaborate trap for you in New Orleans, when I could kill you cheaply right here. Besides the Amateur Mafia sincerely doesn't want you dead. Not at the moment anyway."

"Anything else you want to chat about?"

"No, we've covered about everything. My mother would enjoy having you stay to dinner, if you'll change your mind about your taking off."

"I'm overdue in New Orleans," said Jake. "You have quite a few skycars out on your landing field. I need one."

"Certainly, take your pick," offered Thatcher.

"Bobby, it's dark!" a voice came booming out of the dark palm trees overhead. "You know it's not wise to hunt after sundown! Too dangerous!"

"My mother." Thatcher aimed his rifle at the loudspeaker hanging from one of the jungle trees.

"She worries a good deal about me. Is your mother still among the living?"

"No."

"There's something to be said for that," said Thatcher.

Chapter 7

———◆———

Gunther Stool squinted. "I'm getting very strange interference on my end, Jake," he said out of the pixphone. "A sort of many-colored snow."

"That's confetti," explained Jake.

"Oh, yes, of course. You're in New Orleans and it's always Mardi Gras time there," said the Secretary of Show Biz. "Didn't realize you were outdoors, would have guessed you were indoors."

"I am. My room sends down a shower of confetti from the ceiling every fifteen minutes," explained Jake, brushing off his shoulders.

"What an exciting life you lead," said Stool with a touch of sincere envy. "Kidnapped by the Amateur Mafia, staying in a hotel where they dump confetti on—"

"I wasn't kidnapped. I voluntarily kept the appointment with Bobby Thatcher."

"Didn't mean to imply you were . . . um, Jake, is there a red dot on your nose or should I adjust my phone?"

Flicking a fleck of crimson confetti from the tip of his nose, Jake said, "Bobby Thatcher swears he and the AM have nothing to do with these show business murders, Gunther."

"What would you expect a notorious crook like Thatcher to claim?"

49

"I've got somebody digging into AM secrets," said Jake. "But, tentatively anyway, I believe him."

"You do? Where does that leave us?"

"Have you heard anything about a split in the AM ranks? Thatcher seems to be afraid a splinter group is developing."

"He's putting the blame on this alleged faction?" Stool's jowls flapped when he shook his head. "Sounds like nothing more than a classic piece of buck passing to me. Nonetheless I'll, cautiously, see if the Feds have anything on such a possibility. By the way, has Wildcat intruded into your sphere as yet?"

"Not so far."

"Could be he's tailing Hildy, since he's somewhat miffed at your breaking his leg."

"It was his arm, and I only sprained the damn thing for him," said Jake. "He'd better not try anything cute with Hildy."

"What's your charming wife been able to learn in Switzerland?"

"Can't get in touch with her, she's not at her hotel right now."

"It's past three AM over there, little late for a girl to be—"

"Hildy is not your ordinary girl," Jake reminded him.

"Didn't mean to imply she was. Yet sometimes even the most exceptional people slip. Not that I expect her to—"

"Have you found out anything else I ought to know, Gunther?"

"The Federal Police haven't been able as yet to discover how your flame assassin of yesterday left his asylum. It's almost as though he teleported out."

"That's a possibility," said Jake, nodding.

"Cosmo Ewing could have worked a stunt like that, except he's dead and gone, too."

"What about Shocker Fulson? I'm going to check out the details of his cremation, but has anyone come up with anything?"

Stool told him, "The Federal Police, and they had to go to a Supreme Court robot to get the authorization, opened up Fulson's urn in the Louisiana Habitual Criminal Memorial Park. There were human ashes in there, Jake. They requisitioned a Dr. Spurgeon Mamlish, the gentleman who runs the mortuary which did the job. They hinted to me, without admitting it outright, a little illegal truth juice may have been used on Mamlish. At any rate, the man swears he saw Shocker Fulson's body go sliding into the fiery furnace. So where does that leave us?"

"People are spending money, big money, on this business," Jake said to the Secretary of Show Biz. "Wouldn't cost very much to 'wash Dr. Mamlish so he thinks he saw what he says he saw. Most Fed drugs and devices aren't sophisticated enough to break through a high class 'wash job." He scanned the ceiling. "Going to sign off now, Gunther. I want to miss the next fall of confetti." Jake switched off the pixphone, left his chair and went striding out of his room a step ahead of the multicolored shower.

Chapter 8

———◆———

The straight jacket was one of those talking kind. Made of tough durafibre, designed to soothe, cajole or reprimand the patient. "Don't struggle so, relax. Going to hurt yourself."

Hildy Pace got out of it six minutes after she awakened to find herself restrained. The straight jacket's pleas and threats didn't distract the tall red-haired woman from getting rapidly shed of the thing. Two summers before she'd met Jake, her last year in college, Hildy'd toured New England as assistant to a vaudeville escape artist. She still retained all she'd learned.

"Nasty, bad behavior! Mustn't do this!" warned the straight jacket's tiny speaker as Hildy tossed it aside. "I'm going to yell for . . . awk!"

The heel of her boot ground the speaker mechanism to metallic-plastic grit.

Hands on hips, Hildy surveyed her cell. And it was a cell, no doubting that. The walls had no windows and were covered with cushioned white noryl plastic panels. The white metal door had no handle on this side, the small breakproof-neoglass window was crisscrossed with metal struts. The room, like almost all cells everywhere, was not warm enough and smelled strongly of disinfecting spray.

"That political prison in Morocco was warm," Hildy reminded herself. "Blistering hot, in fact, though Jake wouldn't admit it. Temperatures that high seem to make him cranky."

She made a swift circuit of the room. It was ten feet by twelve feet. Fairly roomy as cells go.

She didn't spot any cameras or bugs, but that didn't mean they were watching her. They probably had more than that little window for observation.

"Maybe I shouldn't have killed the jacket so fast. It might have been able to tell me a little about where the hell I am."

She felt fairly certain she hadn't been unconscious for more than five or six hours. You couldn't always trust those feelings. Hildy was also pretty sure she was still in Switzerland, that she hadn't been carried out of the country while sleeping her drugged sleep.

After one more quick look around, she sat on the chill white floor to tug off her left boot. There was no furniture whatsoever in the cell.

"Thorough, very thorough." Whoever'd dumped her in here, and she had a notion who it was, had found the concealed compartment built into the instep of her boot. The lockpick and tiny laserod had been taken. "Possibly not thorough enough."

With the fingernail of her little finger Hildy drew an invisible picture of a daisy across the bottom of the empty compartment. A click resulted. In the second compartment hidden beneath the first rested another pick and another laserod. Hildy shook those into her hand, slipped her boot back on.

Kneeling, she faced the door. There was absolutely no lock or hint of one on her side of the thick door. No hinges either. "Well, so much for subtlety."

Standing, Hildy flicked on the laserod and sliced the cell door in half across the middle. She then sliced it lengthwise. A heavy kick caused the now quartered door to open out like a blossoming flower.

A quite large man in a one-piece white medsuit was running down the corridor toward her. "You're supposed to stay in your room, Miss Einfuhr," he admonished in English.

"Feeling a bit . . . woozy." She stumbled, genuflected on the white corridor flooring.

The guard was taken in. "Well, no wonder. Busting through a heavy door like that . . . Yike!"

She'd brought her pretty red head right up into his groin. Popping to her feet, she gave him five rapid chops to the neck with the side of her hand.

Dodging the unconscious man's falling body, she ran down the long white hall. At its end a single high window showed a greyish Swiss dawn.

Hoot! Hoot! Hoot!

Something back in her cell was making noise.

Hildy pushed her way through a door labeled, in German, French and English, *Maximum Security Insanity*.

Beyond the door dropped a curving white ramp. Hildy ran down that, since a look out the corridor window as she sprinted by had showed she was up on the fifth floor at least.

Hoot! Hoot!

Another alarm from up in Maximum Security Insanity.

Three floors farther down Hildy came to a door marked *Minimum Security Insanity*.

"This sounds a bit more friendly," she decided.

"And I don't think I can ramp all the way to the ground floor before somebody spots me."

In the corridor she found herself in there were several people, all looking curious about the hooting alarm but none of them officials. A fat man in one-piece rainbow pajamas, staring out of his room. Two women in servochairs wheeling cautiously nearer to her. A thin black man in a cloaklike bathrobe lounging near a room doorway. And, directly in her path a very old man with an immense white beard was spread out flat on his back.

"Need any help?" Hildy asked.

"Can you think of any good ways for getting out of a haunted light house?" the old man asked.

"Several."

He sat up. "Then you can help me plot the—"

"You oughtn't to rise, Mr. Cheektowaga," cautioned one of the servochair women.

"Is he too ill to move?" Hildy asked, with an anxious glance over her shoulder.

No sign of pursuit yet.

"He's plotting," explained the woman.

"I'm the wellknown Claude H. Cheektowaga, Jr." said the old man. "I always plot this way, flat on my ass. Got into the habit in 1923 in Alaska. Found myself flat on my ass, due primarily to a sock on the snoot delievered by a very tricky Eskimo, and while I was stretched out an idea came to me. *The Tuffy Twins in the Haunted House.* It's sold 9,000,000 copies to date and formed the cornerstone of the entire Tuffy Twins series."

"And the cause," said the other chaired woman, "of your being stuck here in the Famous Artists Madhouse."

"True, true," acknowledged the semi-prone author. "The royalties on my Tuffy Twins are such that my relatives, and there are hundreds of the buggers if you count all the great great grandchildren, were inspired to—"

"They got control of his rights and dumped him here," said the black man. "Much the same as my kin did to me. I'm Yolan Gentz, creator of the Moderate Man comic books. Why'd *your* relatives stick you here?"

Hoot! Hoot! Hoot!

"Do any of you," Hildy asked the minimum security patients, "have rooms with windows?"

"I do," said Gentz, "being an artist and needing north light."

Edging around the Tuffy Twins author, Hildy went into the black man's room. There was a large window, protected only by three fragile-seeming bars. It wasn't even smashproof glass. "This should be close enough to the ground for—"

All at once the window exploded in at her. Shards of glass and twists of bar came flying into the room.

"Don't spill my ink," cried Gentz.

The cause of the breaking glass and twisting metal was a large blond man in a single-piece burgundy tracksuit. He'd come sailing through the window, clutching the end of a rope. He let go of the rope, smacked down onto the artist's bed, which was stacked high with faxprint comic books.

"Those are priceless, some of them!" Gentz shouted. "Do you know the Overstreet value of early Moderate Mans?"

"An impressive entrance, huh?" The big man asked Hildy as he bounced off the bed amid flying comic books. He hit the floor with an impressive thunk.

Hildy thrust the laserod out where he could see

it. "Out of my way, Wildcat! I'm going to avail myself of the opening your oafish carcass has—"

"Unk!" Unexpectedly he kicked up. His boot toe crunched into Hildy's fingers, sending the rod spinning.

The laserod banged the wall, spurted on briefly and sliced the drawing board neatly in half.

Lars "Wildcat" Brasher was on his feet now, standing in his familiar expectant gorilla stance. He smiled at Hildy. "You got to admit I'm smart, Hilda. Minute I saw you breaking out of your cell, I guessed what floor you'd hit for. Yup, that I did."

"There goes my chance for a comeback," lamented the black artist. "You people have chopped my latest Moderate Man splash page right in two. I spent five grueling days penciling in all those werewolves gnawing at the base of the—"

"You jumped me in the street," Hildy said to Wildcat.

"Yup. Jake Pace couldn't have done it smoother," the Federal Police agent boasted.

This reminds me very much of *The Tuffy Twins in the Haunted Dog & Cat Hospital*," old bewhiskered Cheektowaga was saying out in the hall. "Also a bit of *The Tuffy Twins in the Haunted Lumber Yard*."

"Don't go ogling the window so lovingly, Hilda," said Wildcat. "The staff'll be here in a mo to toss you into an even tougher cell."

"Eventually Jake'll spring me, if I can't myself. So what's the—"

"The purpose, Hilda, is to keep you out of the way while I solve this god damn murder case."

"Locking me in a madhouse won't keep my husband from beating you to it."

"Ha ha," laughed Wildcat. "Jake I don't have to

worry about no more. He won't sprain anymore of my ankles."

"It was your arm, and he broke it," said Hildy. "What do you mean?"

"The opposition, and I know a couple things about them you don't, got a little trap planned for Jake way down yonder in New Orleans. Ha ha." Wildcat thumped his broad chest a few times.

"People are always laying snares for Jake, but he doesn't often get caught."

"He'll get caught in this one," Wildcat assured her with a few more boisterous chest thumps. "You want to know why? Because he won't be able to keep from walking right into it. If you want to catch yourself a Jake Pace you got to appeal to his vanity."

"Jake's not vain." Hildy was, apparently without thinking about it, swinging her lockpick back and forth in her hand. "He isn't vain at all."

"Isn't vain at all." Wildcat was watching the bright object go ticking from side to side. "Isn't vain at all."

"You, on the other hand, are awfully sleepy," Hildy told the giant government agent. "Very sleepy, and why not since it's so early in the morning."

"Yup, I could use a good snooze right about . . ." He wilted down to the floor.

"Astounding," said Gertz. "Even Moderate Man, with his Electric Zen powers, couldn't have—"

"This trap," Hildy said when she bent over the hypnotized Wildcat, "for Jake in New Orleans . . . what is it?"

"Vanity, vanity," murmured Brasher.

"In there! She's in there!"

Official voices, official footsteps. Coming closer.

Making a disappointed sound, Hildy ran to the window and looked down. There was a rooftop ten feet below. She jumped.

Chapter 9

———◆———

Jean Lafitte said, "Stirfry unger marble zonga verble waffle."

"I didn't quite catch that," admitted Jake.

"It's because of this damn cutlass," said the man in the pirate costume after removing the sword from between his teeth. "Nobody seems to understand me when I got it clutched between the old pearlies."

Sigmund Freud, Gene Autry and Robinson Crusoe came rollicking down the sidewalk arm in arm.

Jake stepped out of their way. "Where can I find him?" he asked the pirate's left ear, the one with the gold ring in it.

Exploding firecrackers prevented his hearing the reply.

Carmen Miranda staggered by on the arm of Horatio Hornblower.

"Not the best corner for a quiet meeting," Jake said to his contact.

"Furble the postern . . . excuse it. This sort of meet fools the opposition. Nobody'd suspect a clandestine get-together right out in the open during the nightly Mardi Gras parade."

"Okay, where's Steranko the Siphoner?"

"He's got himself a new underground—"

"The King of the Sulus!"

"Here he comes now!"

Woodrow Wilson, Margaret Truman, Robin Hood, Esther Williams and Charles A. Lindbergh stopped to join the parade-watching crowd on Jake's corner. They were quite excited about the approaching parade float.

"Sometimes," said Lafitte, "you can get damn tired of Mardi Gras. Long about August you feel, 'If I see that flapping King of the Sulus roll by one more time, I'll—' "

"Where can I find him?"

"He's got a new layout, all underground," replied the pirate. "There's got to be more money in Steranko's line of work than in the paid stooge field. He's got an impressive damn setup. What's a man to do, though? I consulted a personnel guidance computer once and my aptitudes suited me for A. Paid Stooge, B. Toady and C—"

"Where the hell is Steranko? Specifically."

"Under Zombie Village. Ask for the hardware department, that's your password. Didn't I tell you the address already? Yeah, I did, but it was while I was chomping on the sword. The third choice was C. Dutiful Minion. Some selection to guide your life by."

"Obviously you're meant for better things." Passing him a folded $20 bill, Jake moved away through the costumed crowd.

"Watch it, jerkoff," complained Charles Dickens as Jake pushed by him.

Zombie Village was a new club on Rampart Street. When Jake reached its rattan doors they burst open to allow Zorro, Tarzan and Emily

Brontë to be heaved out into the night by a blank-
eyed zombie.

"Who're you supposed to be?" Tarzan asked
Jake while extricating himself from the gutter.

"That's not much of a costume," said Emily
Brontë, scrutinizing him.

"Actually it's allegorical," he said, treating the
three of them to a bleak smile. "I'm the Spirit of a
Punch in the Nose."

"Troublemaker," decided Zorro, who'd finally
succeeded in locating his sword. "Let's go over to
the Jass Museum, kids. I believe the Al Hirt robot's
playing there tonight."

"I love him," said Emily Brontë. "I love all fat
robots."

"He's an android," clarified Zorro.

Jake pushed on into the dimlit club. The decor
suggested a Haitian jungle. Up on a dirt-covered
bandstand a naked black girl was decapitating a
chicken.

"No seating during this act," a zombie whis-
pered.

"I'm looking for the hardware department," Jake
told the seven-foot-tall Scandinavian.

"You're apparently misguided, sir. You're in a
night club. Now for hardware you—"

"It's a password. See, I come in and say to you
that—"

"EEK!"

"Calm yourself, Madeleine. It's only—"

"Eek! Eek!"

At a table near the bandstand a blonde woman
had started jumping up and down. Her escort was
trying to persuade her to sit again.

"A chicken head landing right in my lap. How
discomforting."

"It's not a real chicken head, Madeleine. See? It's stuffed with plyocelsior."

"I can't stand excelsior touching my body. Don't let it get all over my thighs and kneecaps."

"I'm looking for the hardware department," Jake tried again on his zombie.

The tall man gave himself a clout in the head with the heel of his hand. "Oh, yes, I remember now. I don't know, being a zombie seems to affect my thinking processes. Come right this way."

He led Jake across a grassy clearing, past a cluster of voodoo drummers and along a tree-lined corridor.

"Actually I'm darn lucky to be a zombie at all," the blond man confided. "It's tough for a Swede to get hired for such a job, since zombies are traditionally black. You want that door over there, sir, with the juju hanging on it. Knock thrice . . . no, it's four times. Do you know the correct form for that? I mean there's once, twice, thrice . . . and then what?"

Jake left his escort to knock four times on the door.

"Yeah?" asked a reedy voice on the other side.

"Hardware department," said Jake.

"How's that again?"

"I'm looking for the hardware department, and I'm coming to feel damn silly about it."

"That could only be the wiseass Jake Pace, using his feeble wits to hide his confusion. Enter, old pal."

The door clicked, swung outward. A pinkish twist of floating lightstrips illuminated a steeply inclining ramp going down into darkness.

Jake went down the ramp.

"Still underweight I see. You know why? You're

hyperactive. Sure, all you daredevils are. Run, jump, hop, skip. Never sit still, too arrogant to rely on machines. Burns up your flesh. Supposed to be good for the heart and respiration. Do you know, though, how many jockstraps kick off before the age of fifty every year?"

"Must be upwards of a hundred," Jake said into the musky dark at the ramp bottom.

"Over this way, over this way. You're supposed to be terrific at finding your way around in the pitch dark. Didn't you once chase a vampire through the sewers of Paris?"

"It was a gorilla with a human brain," Jake told his still unseen questioner. "It was up the side of the Revised Eiffel Tower at a few minutes past noon."

"Can't believe that, because I have more info about you at my fingertips than any other private or public info retrieval service in the world. Sit down."

Light blossomed. A metal door slid shut behind Jake.

Steranko the Siphoner was seated in a real wood rocker. A small man, not more than five foot three, wearing a lemon yellow one-piece laxsuit. He was in his late twenties, completely bald. All around them rose electronic equipment and media gear, piled and stacked in a pattern which was rational only to Steranko. Ball TVs floated at various levels, monitor screens were built into the wall and ceiling, with even a few image screens underfoot. "How's your gawky wife?"

"As well as can be expected."

"More pallid whimsy," said Steranko in his high piping voice. "$2,000."

"Same to you." Jake placed his backside on the edge of a slightly lopsided datadesk.

"That's my fee, wisenheimer." The small hand he held out was covered with a lemon yellow glove. "You haven't commented on my new suit or my new headquarters."

"Layout's cluttered, as always. Suit's a size too small, or possibly you're a size too big. Do you really have $2000 worth of information for me?"

"I charge some people that much just to kiss my bummy."

"The government ought to step in and put on price controls." Jake's hand, when it reappeared from under his tunic held two folded $1000 bills.

"Notice what you're almost sitting on, Jake? It's the latest Tex Instrument computer sife."

Jake patted the lunchbox-sized instrument. "I heard this was still in the experimental stage."

"It is, that's one of the test models." He leaned out in his rocker, snatching the cash from Jake. "Did you see your horsey wife on the tube today. No, I guess you don't catch Swiss TV." He pointed at one of the floating television sets.

A full-color picture appeared. There was Hildy, Greta and the other two nude members of the *Naked Shadows* string quartet playing.

"Look what your wife's got to do to earn your bread, Jake. Parade around with her equipment hanging out on display. What a life."

Jake's grin broadened. "You'll have to make me a copy of that."

"$120."

"Now what about the Amateur Mafia?"

"Simpletons." He reached under his chair to jab at a button on a control panel which had been tossed there.

Out of a loudspeaker hidden from sight in a welter of equipment voices came.

". . . mother doesn't like it either."

"We can't get a damn thing, Bobby."

"Aren't we the Amateur Mafia? We're powerful . . . what's that, Mom? Mom says we're the most powerful crime syndicate ever known. Still we can't find out who's killing these entertainers."

"We've got our best men in DC, out on the Coast, all over. I put six info centers to work on the problem. Nothing but dead ends so . . ."

Steranko said, "I can play you several hours of similar tripe. It's not shuck stuff, they weren't doing an act for anyone's benefit. The AM really doesn't know who's been killing show biz nebbishes."

"Do you?"

"Not for a pissing $2000."

"Do you know?"

"I can find out, Jake. Sitting right here I can solve this mess a lot faster than you and your barnstorming frau can by barging around all over the world."

Jake asked, "What about the real Mafia? Could this be part of a comeback bid?"

"Good query." Steranko swung a yellow-booted foot out to flip a toggle on a panel leaning against a mid-20th century movieola.

Up near the ceiling one of the TV screens flashed on.

"Okay, okay, I'll tell you!" A dark-haired young man, face bloody, was backed against a candy-striped wall. "It might be . . . it . . . ah . . ."

"Stupid cluck, you killed him."

"Okay, so sometimes that happens."

"He was going to tell us things."

"I beat him a bit too good. We'll have to find us another Mafioso."

Two men, wide backs to the hidden camera, were standing over the newly dead Mafia man.

"There is a link. He was going to tell us about it."

The picture faded out.

"That is about as far as the AM has gone in tying the oldtime Mafia to this caper," said Steranko the Siphoner.

"Keep digging on that angle," said Jake. "At the usual rates."

"Got something else for you," said the information expert. "Nobody knows this, save me and my gadgets. Reason being the Feds and the AM let a few simple 'puter blocks fool them. Who took care of Shocker Fulson's funeral and cremation?"

"A Dr. Spurgeon Mamlish."

"Wrong again. All that info is diversion feed, put into all the significant 'puter systems by a very clever operator. So clever, to give you a better notion, even I haven't been able to trace him. Yet."

Jake swung off the desk. "Who did get Shocker's body?"

"It was shipped, via skyvan, to New Iberia, Louisiana. To a branch of Doc Inferno. You familiar with Doc Inferno?"

"Nationwise cremation service, got a hundred or more branches. What did their New Iberia branch do with Shocker?"

"Go find out." His elbow threw another switch.

On a TV set floating quite near to Jake's head a picture appeared. A field of ripe grain swayed in a gentle summer wind. "Thanks, America, for taking us to your heart. We love you, too. We love, when that terrible moment comes, to dispose of your loved ones cheaply and efficiently. And Doc Inferno is cheap. Did you know you can have as many as three loved ones—so long as it's at one and the same time—you can have up to three loved ones incinerated at the same time and take advantage of Doc's Big Burner Plan. Right. We'll cremate up to three loved ones at any of our 197 Doc Inferno Parlors and . . . get this! You give us $1000 and we'll give you back change." The commercial ended with the field starting to burn.

"Who owns the Doc Inferno business?" Jake asked.

"Used to be the real Mafia controlled it. May still be the case, but they've got it set up in a very tricky way. I'm in the process of finding out," said Steranko. "Here's some advice I'll give you direct from me, no tapes or films involved. People have ended up in urns after a visit to a Doc Inferno Parlor. People who went in alive and kicking."

"I'll remember that when I visit New Iberia," said Jake. "Do you know a girl in town named Quebec?"

"Too skinny." His left hand turned a knob on a nearby control board.

On the floor a view screen came to life. A pretty Negro girl was sitting on a floating loveseat, toying with the glowtrim of her one-piece lace lingeriesuit. "We don't get many calls for ten-year-old boys at this outlet, Mr. *Bonk!*"

"Quebec, I might be able to make do with an eleven-year-old if he's not too . . . developed. Do you get my drift?"

"By now there's hardly a drift I don't get, Mr. *Bonk!* I think you'd be better off trying . . ."

Steranko killed the film. "Grand jury tape made five months ago," he said. "Which is why the john's name is deleted. It's Roland Mott, of the National Starvation Study Group, if you're interested."

"I'm not. Know where I can find Quebec?"

"I can find out."

"Might have you do that later. First I'll talk to Swan."

Steranko laughed. "Paddlewheel Swan? If that simp hadn't wed Thatcher's cousin, he'd be polishing andies down in the bayou."

"The Quebec girl supposedly had a lead on what really happened to Shocker Fulson. She was going to come up to tell Swan, disappeared instead."

"Logical."

"Why logical?"

"Could be Swan isn't 100 percent loyal to AM. They don't know that as yet, but I do. You going to visit him on the riverboat?"

"When we part."

"Noisy place, all those android replicas of last-century jazz bands. Do you like that kind of music?"

"My musical tastes are catholic, running from android jazz to naked Mozart."

"I've had enough of the fabled Pace wit for one night, Jake," Steranko informed him. "You've had more than $2000 worth of exclusive info. Goodbye."

"I'll check with you again before I leave town." Jake headed for the door.

"If you remain alive."

Chapter 10

"Isn't that amazing?" asked Swan.

"Not especially," replied Jake.

"I find it highly amazing." The chubby blond man rolled the unlit cigarette between his pale chubby fingers. "Who would think you could become addicted to an old fashioned vice like tobacco? Yet here I am puffing away on a whole pack a day, which amounts to 20 cigs. You can't even buy the darn things with ease. Government outlawed them years ago, all the legit tobacco growers switched over to junk food. If it weren't for the bootleggers down in Red Cuba I'd be shit out of luck." He lit his tobacco cigarette. "Does tobacco smoke bother you?"

"Yeah."

"I'll attempt to exhale discreetly then." After a long satisfying puff, the manager of the Jazzboat relaxed in his aluminum swivel chair. "Does being over the water bother you?"

The paddlewheeler was moored at the edge of an artificial lagoon.

"Not at all," said Jake. "Where do you think the girl Quebec is?"

"Haven't the faintest idea." He rested his chubby elbows on his tin desk. "Do you know anything about the side effects of tobacco? I don't mean cancer and heart disease. What I'm starting to worry about is maybe tobacco dims your wits and curbs your curiosity. I find I don't care a fig about the fate of little Quebec. Being a slave to Lady Nicotine has—"

"Quebec called you. Where was she, what did she hint she knew?"

Swan puffed again, allowed the smoke to spill out over his fat slightly pouty lower lip. "The kid was on a recruiting trip for her houses. Very gifted young lady, eighteen and managing three full-time bordellos."

"Puts her in line for a Junior Achievement award. Where exactly was she when she last contacted you?"

"Around New Iberia I do believe."

"She'd heard something about Shocker Fulson."

"Did you know Shocker? A wonderfully gifted fellow, but a lout." After a few more inhalations of tobacco smoke, Swan went on. "I really, Mr. Pace, don't know much beyond what you've already been told."

"Thatcher implied you did."

"Bobby tends to overrate me, since I had the good judgment to marry into the family."

A knock sounded on the office door, then a very pretty blonde girl entered. "Forgive me for intruding." She was tall, as tall as Hildy, and dressed in a low-front two-piece bizsuit. "I was given to understand, Mr. Swan, that a Jake Pace was visiting you."

"He is, Mindy Sue. This is Jake Pace you see before you."

Mindy Sue smiled, at the same time fisting herself below her breasts to indicate pleasure and excitement. "What a pleasure to meet you, Mr. Pace, sir." She held out the hand she'd just used for thumping.

Jake rose to shake it. "Well, thanks, Mindy Sue."

"I'm hoping I can impose on you."

"Now, Mindy Sue," warned the chubby Jazzboat manager, "Mr. Pace is in New Orleans on important business which—"

"What do you want?" Jake asked the big pretty girl.

"You know how androids are. Well sir, our Jelly Roll Morton & His Red Hot Peppers android band is due to perform in less than ten minutes and wouldn't you know it Jelly Roll Morton is malfunctioning."

"Maybe I can fix him if you—"

"No, no, Mr. Pace, I doubt even your very nimble fingers and lightning-swift brain can mend him in time to save us from disappointing our large audience on Deck A," said Mindy Sue, somewhat breathless. "What I had in mind . . . would you sit in?"

"Play piano in your Morton andy's place?"

"Oh, yes, exactly. I just know, having heard so very much about your musical gifts, you'll do—"

"As a matter of fact, I do play jazz piano pretty well. Not quite up to being an original, but I can always do a fair imitation of the greats like Art Tatum, Speckled Red, Champion Jack Dupree, Bud Powell, James P. Johnson—"

"Oh, oh, those names are all near and dear to me, as they should be to anyone who's going to manage the shows for the Jazzboat." gasped Mindy Sue. "Will you?" She tugged hopefully on his arm.

"Sure. If it's okay with Swan."

Swan coughed. "An honor is what you'd be bestowing on the Jazzboat, Mr. Pace."

Jake allowed himself to be guided out of the office, across the lower deck of the renovated riverboat and up to A Deck.

Nearly sixty people, many in costume, were seated at checkered tables out on the moonlit deck. On a square elevated stage the android New Orleans Rhythm Kings were completing *Clarinet Marmalade*.

"I'm fantastically excited by this decision of yours," Mindy Sue told Jake with her lovely face inches from his. "You're married, aren't you?"

"I am, yes."

"How completely? I mean, when I feel this elated by someone it's sort of a custom of mine to jump into the sack with him. Would your wife mind something like that?"

"Check with me after the show." Jake was watching the NORK group bow and leave the stage.

"Of course, of course. I don't want you to become all horny and sexually stimulated and tumescent. That will detract from your performance possibly, although my reading in the jazz archives leads me to believe many of the jazz immortals were . . . well, you'd best let me sneak you around backstage. It's nearly time."

"Are your androids programmed to do a specific set of tunes?"

"No, you can call the shots, Mr. Pace. May I call you Jake? I'm so heightened by you and what you're doing for me. It seems silly to be thinking about bedding down with you in scant minutes and yet still calling you Mr. Pace. Although I'm given to understand that in certain AM bordellos a practice of that sort of formality is conducive to—"

"So call me Jake," he said. "We'll start with a slow one."

"In bed? It's entirely up—"

"On the bandstand. We'll do *Someday Sweetheart* for the opening number, I'll do a little badinage with the andies and we'll swing into *Sidewalk Blues*. If that goes over with your audience I'll try a couple of the Morton piano solos, *The Pearls* and possibly *Naked Dance*."

"Oh oh," Mindy Sue fairly moaned, "that would be exciting beyond belief. If you solo I may just charge the stand and ball you right then and there."

"Best wait until the set concludes, Mindy Sue. There's an old show business taboo about breaking into somebody else's act."

They were behind the stage now, among the silent android members of the Red Hot Pepper group. The Jelly Roll Morton andy was slumped in a corner, winking, smirking and snapping its fingers. The diamond set in his front tooth sparkled.

"You're on, Jake." Mindy Sue gave his private parts an encouraging clutch. "Get out there and wow them, as I know you will."

An unseen announcer announced, "Now, moldy figs and gutbucket buffs, we offer you our meticulous recreation of one of the greatest New Orleans jazz bands of the last century. Jelly Roll Morton & His Red Hot Peppers. With, as a once in a lifetime special treat, that noted daredevil investigator Jake Pace of Odd Jobs, Inc. sitting in for Mr. Morton, who is malfunctioning tonight."

The androids followed Jake up the stairway which led out to the bandstand.

The ovation he got as he stepped into the limelight was gratifying. Hildy, on occasion, chided him for being vain about his musical abilities. But if you're gifted, you have to accept it.

The first number, the slow ballad *Someday Sweetheart*, went over very well. The audience looked to be on the verge of a standing ovation.

"They probably don't toss the Morton android this sort of reaction," he said to himself. Putting his fingers to his lips he gave a whistle. "Hey, get on out the way! You want to knock the streetcar off the tracks?" he called to the Kid Ory android. "You so dumb you ought to be president of the deaf and dumb society."

"I'm sorry, boss," responded the trombonist andy, "but I got the Sidewalk Blues."

Then Jake started playing, the Ory android came in, followed by the other members of the group.

At this juncture the front row customers stood up at their tables. Marlene Dietrich, Batman, Erich Fromm, Fu Manchu, Shirley Temple, Martin Luther, Wendell Wilkie and a Norwegian man who probably wasn't in costume.

"A little soon for a standing ovation on this tune," Jake reflected as he chopped out Morton style piano.

He realized what they had in mind about ten seconds too late.

Each of the standing figures had whipped out a stungun.

Jake was only halfway off the piano stool when several stun beams hit him. The Norwegian man missed.

Chapter 11

"Well, she broke all my fingers, broke all my toes.

Yeah, my baby broke all my fingers, then she broke my toes.

I was in such a bad shape, I couldn't even thumb my nose.

Well, she—"

"This isn't the time for that, Red."

"Always time for the blues. You gets up in the morning, you is got 'em. You eats some granola an' there they is, you—"

"For a guy who graduated from Peanut Tech in Georgia, Red, you sure have a funny way of talking."

"Peanuts ain't exactly culture, Quebec. 'Sides, I is so steeped in the blues, well, I just natural talk something like a 20th-century bluesman."

"Let's give this poor guy a chance to wake up peaceable."

Jake added visual impressions to the audio ones he'd been receiving for the past few minutes. He saw a spread of carpet, old and worn, a boot tapping the dust out of the threadbare rug, an attractive bare black leg. He saw his own left hand and . . . yeah, over here was his right. An initial attempt to use them to push himself, or even his head, off the tacky rug was unsuccessful.

"He's trying to get up, Red. Help him."

"Ain't hardly no sense in that, Quebec. Gets up and he gonna see what a mean old world this is. Gonna see how death is always standin' 'bout two paces hind of your coattails waiting—"

"Shit, I'll do it. Easy now, Pace." A cool hand took hold of his arm, lifted.

The visual impressions went fuzzy. His stomach lurched, growled. "Not quite . . . so . . . fast."

"I hear they used half a dozen stunners on you." Quebec eased him to his knees.

"Thereabouts," he answered in a muddy voice. "Vanity . . . vanity . . ."

"That's right, bubber," said Red. "Whole round world ain't nothing else but."

"No more philosophy till he's got his bearings, Red."

Jake could see a wooden chair now, a sprung sofa, a terrible floor lamp with a shade immortalizing an 18th-century naval battle, some kind of sandwich-making appliance resting on a lopsided table. The remoter sections of the room stayed blurry. "How . . . long . . ."

"I can do that one," volunteered Red. "Baby, tell me how long has—"

"How long . . . have I been . . . here?"

"About sixteen hours," Quebec informed him. "They really stunned you something fierce."

Jake, with considerable help from the Negro girl, reached the sofa. "Sixteen, huh? Long time . . ." He sat.

"Long time to be sleeping on somebody else's floor."

"Been a long time, baby, since I had my meat-grinder fixed,

It's been a long time—"

"Hold off for a while, Red. Jake Pace, this is Nearsighted Red, the noted, if you ain't guessed already, blues singer."

Jake was concentrating on breathing, carefully, in and out. "You knew . . . my name."

"That's on account of Two-Ton," explained the girl. "He's one of our what you might call jailers."

"Where exactly are we?"

"This is the New Iberia branch Doc Inferno Parlor. We're down underground."

"Everybody's going underground," muttered Jake. "Have you been here since you disappeared?"

"I have, along with Nearsighted Red."

"I weren't doing nothin' cept being a ninnocent bystander," said the freckled black young man while trying a few blue chords on his steel body guitar.

"Red had the misfortune to be my customer when I was grabbed," Quebec explained. "I was working in our newest teen brothel in these parts. Really more of a shakedown cruise than any real interest in turning tricks. Then in pops Two-Ton with a couple of husky morticians."

Jake discovered he could see the entire room. The final traces of the stunning were fading. "Who's this Two-Ton work for?"

Quebec bit her lip. "I tell you all I know, you're gonna be in as big trouble as me."

"We all gwine be toasted," Red reminded. "We all prime contenders for occupation of urns. Don't make no never mind what you tells this joker."

Sighing, the girl nodded. "Two-Ton's a longtime customer of mine, too," she began. "Started patronizing me when I was fourteen up in New Orleans. Whenever I'm down here I—"

"Too long, too long, my baby always talk too long.

By the time she tell me something I been and gone."

"I'm telling the story my way, Red." Quebec seated herself beside the recuperating Jake. "Unfortunately, or maybe fortunately should we get out of this mess alive, Two-Ton is the kind of customer who likes to confide. He's been working at this Doc Inferno parlor since it opened two three years ago." She rubbed her palms along her inner thighs, taking a breath. "Me being liked by him is why we're still not nothing but soot, and why we get to eat regular." She gestured toward the sandwichbox.

Jake said, "Two-Ton must have told you about Shocker Fulson, how Doc Inferno here handled the body."

Quebec said, "And I made the mistake of telling Swan."

"Yeah, he's obviously on some other side. Now what about Shocker's body?"

"That body was never cremated, instead they froze it and shipped it somewheres else."

"Where?"

"Two-Ton never told me, but he knows. I was planning to find out, but got snatched up instead," said Quebec. "Does the name Patchwork mean anything to you?"

"Not as yet. Why?"

"Shocker's body was going to end up with a person who's known as Patchwork."

"Patchwork," said Jake. "Swan may know."

"That bastard. I pixphone him and that very night they come for me."

"An me," added Red.

Jake got up, unaided, off the swayback sofa. Walking with increasing confidence, he explored the room, kicked at the baseboards, thumping the walls, tromping on the floor. "Metal floors and walls under all these schlubby rugs and dimwitted wallpaper. Door's solid steel, too, painted to look like wood."

"Se we noticed," said Red.

Standing still, Jake frisked himself, clothes and footwear. "They appear to have taken all my concealed weapons and tools," he announced after a moment.

"Least they left me my old guitar," mentioned the blues singer.

"There's a possibility," said Jake, grinning down at the instrument.

Chapter 12

"Let's not cremate any more Irishmen for a spell," suggested Boody Lasswell, the proprietor of the New Iberia branch Doc Inferno Parlor. "Them Hibernian wakes take a lot out of a feller." He was a frail man in his late forties, standing in the aftermath of a wake. The afternoon sun glaring on the artificial swamp outside the reception area made his eyes narrow. Corned beef and cabbage splashed on the furniture, empty whisky flasks strewn about, shillalah splinters every whichwhere, little green hats hanging from the light fixtures, shamrocks ground into the thermal carpeting.

"I'll go fetch our clean up 'bot," offered Two-Ton, an immensely fat youth with crinkly blond hair.

"You can't not do that on account of a bunch of them micks rewired him and now instead of sucking up debris and garbage he don't do nothing but sing *When Irish Eyes Are Smiling, A Little Bit of Ireland* and *Little Brown Jug*."

"*Little Brown Jug* ain't an Irish ditty."

"Try telling that to 126 crazed Irishmen."

Two-Ton, grunting and huffing, started gathering up some of the abandoned plaz whisky flasks. "They're a sentimental race," he observed. "Like

81

the way they insisted O'Brien's faithful hound get roasted along with him."

"His dog, two cats and some kind of very strange bird," amplified Lasswell, staring out at the painfully bright afternoon. "We going to have trouble sure if the head office ever finds out. Only one customer to a coffin, that's in the guide book."

Two-Ton unloaded the gathered flasks on a floating table. "Aw, what's a few pets compared to the Shocker Fulson deal?"

"Whoops!" Lasswell's frail body quivered, his arms flapped. "You ain't to allude to that deal, never. We made arrangements with certain parties, Two-Ton, certain parties with certain connections and that's all. You got your share."

"Not bitching about that aspect, Boody." With an enormous grunt the fat youth lowered himself to the rug. "Alls I was trying to point out is a little bird ashes in with Jocko O'Brien is a spit in the bucket when compared with hijacking a corpse and dropping it off on some godforsaken—"

"No more jawing about Shocker Fulson," said the crematorium proprietor. "You want to worry about something, worry about how to get them greeny splotches off the carpets."

"Shamrock green, Boody, that's a mighty hard stain to handle. Already looked her up in my stain removal manual, wherein they advise ignoring it and praying. So I—"

"Shush up a minute."

"Why you cupping your hand to your good ear, Boody?"

"Quiet. I hear something."

With head slightly cocked, Two-Ton listened. "Aw, that's only some jigaboo music, that's all."

"They playing *Didn't He Ramble*." The proprie-

tor made his way through the wake debris to the
seethrough door. "Got to be one of them brass funeral bands wending its way to us."

"We ain't got no jigaboos scheduled to roast until tomorrow morn." Two-Ton, with much chuff-
ing and swaying, returned to his feet. "And that's
Mrs. Claybrook and the only music her kin sprung
for is five minutes of the moog."

"Holy Jesus!"

"Is it sure enough a funeral, Boody? Is that why
you begun praying?"

"I ain't praying. I'm cursing my fate because
coming up the flagstone path to our door at the
head of that procession is Doc."

"Doc who?"

"Well, Doc Inferno, you ninny."

"Doc Inferno. I ain't never seen him save in com-
mercials. He's a real cute little old man, looks
mighty like a jolly Southern colonel. Give me a
peek." He lurched in the direction of the door.

"No time for peeking, you got to clean this darn
parlor," shouted Lasswell, quivering in new spots.
"This got to be one of the unexpected inspections
the guidebook tells about. If Doc Inferno sees this
unholy mess, we'll—"

"How about if he lays eyes on Quebec and
Nearsighted Red and Jake Pace whom we got
snuckered down below? He might dirty his nice
white britches."

"Jesus, Mary and Joseph! I clean forgot we was
holding them for eventual delivery Southward."

Out on the path a little old man, extremely jolly
in mien, was strutting ever closer to the entry. He
was only twenty yards away, at his back a nine-
man uniformed band was marching. At his side

strode a tall redhaired woman in a very sedate one-piece bizsuit.

"I best go down," offered Two-Ton, "and spirit them away."

"Yes, yes. You better, Two-Ton. Be sure they don't scream or holler," said the distraught Lasswell. "Shamrocks and cabbage I can maybe explain, but not screams and hollers."

"Right away." The floor rattled as the giant youth went running from the reception area.

Swallowing, smoothing his clothes, Lasswell stepped a pace forward as the parlor doors automatically snapped open. "As I live and breathe, if it ain't Doc Inferno himself. What a pleasant surprise."

"I could just bong him on the head with the guitar." Nearsighted Red gestured with his recently unstrung instrument. "Thought bout doing that the last time Two-Ton come tom-cattin' around."

"Too blatant." Jake was making a few final adjustments on the sandwichbox. Using nothing but the A and C strings from Red's guitar and his bare hands, he'd made significant modifications in the microwave cooking unit. "There we are. Very few people are aware how simple it is to turn one of these gadgets into a weapon."

"Will it kill him?" Quebec wanted to know.

"I rarely kill people." Jake placed the sandwichbox on the shaky end table next to the ancient sofa. "Besides which Two-Ton knows stuff I want to know."

"This here escape plan," said Red, "seem to me it tend to favor one member of our trio over the others. Mean to say, next time Two-Ton come in to see Quebec we use that thing there to coldcok him. Okay, that part is fine. But then we got to loiter around whiles you quiz him."

"You and Quebec can leave as soon as Two-Ton is out," Jake told him. "There are several skyvans out on the landing ramp, according to Quebec."

"Along with probably a few goons," said the girl. "Three against them is better than two. I'm going to wait until—"

"Troubled times, troubled times." The heavy door of their parlor-like cell rumbled open. Two-Ton barged in with a stungun in his left hand, a blaster pistol in his right. "You all are going to be moving to new quarters."

"I hate moving," said Quebec. "Why we have to?"

"It's on account of Doc Inferno. That cute little old man is right upstairs at this very moment," the immense youth explained. "Won't do to have him notice you folks."

"Doc Inferno isn't on your side in this?" asked Jake, easing back toward the augmented sandwich-box.

"No, he surely isn't. Now gather yourselves together, so as we can sneak out."

Quebec approached Two-Ton. "Don't you even have a little minute to sit and talk. I been looking forward to it a good deal."

"Well now . . ." He smiled at her. Then shuddered, shaking his bulky head. "Out of the question, there ain't time. Doc Inferno accompanied by that whole damn brass band, could come snooping down here any sec—"

"Brass band?" Quebec placed her hand on his fat shoulder. "Did the old gentlemen bring—"

"Aw, now, sweety cake, I truly don't have no time for polite conversation. We got to move."

Jake had placed himself beside the sandwichbox. "Suppose we all commence hollering and shouting? Doc Inferno will hear us."

"I sincerely hope you don't, because then I will shoot each and ever one of you," Two-Ton promised. "I got strict orders not one yelp is to be heard from . . . put that down!"

Jake had lifted up the box. "Don't we get to take a few belongings with us?"

"That ain't hardly yours no how, and even if it—"

Zzzzt! Zizzle!

A peach-color ray shot out of the small front door of the sandwichbox. When it touched Two-Ton's chest he straightened up, mouth dropping open, eyes rolling upward. He thereafter tumbled to his knees.

Jake nudged the fat youth in the side and Two-Ton fell the rest of the way down. It made an impressive thump. "Now to ask some questions."

"You honestly do appear much younger in real life than you do on the TV, Doc."

"Stuff the flattery, Boody," said the white-whiskered gentleman. "You explain how come this reception area is such an allfired mess."

"The Irish," said Lasswell.

Hildy Pace tapped the camera she was holding. "Shall I snap any publicity shots, Doc?" she inquired. "Something with you and Mr. Lasswell shaking hands in a friendly fashion? I believe if you two were to stand over there beneath the light ball which appears to be wearing a green hat I can get a picture which won't even hint at what a sorry mess everything is hereabouts."

"Your band isn't helping anything, Doc," said the

frail Lasswell. "Nine men tramping around on the rugs is only going to rub the shamrocks and cabbage and whatever that organish gunk is deeper into the carpeting. I realize you—"

"Don't go badmouthing the Yreka Brass Band, Lasswell," warned Doc Inferno. "I have plans for them, grandiose plans which may even include night-time television."

"Couldn't they stand at attention or something? At least that way they—"

"They're restless, upset," said the white-suited, white-whiskered man. "Who wouldn't be on entering this . . . this pig sty."

"Your average pig sty doesn't have a blanket of shamrocks underfoot," said Lasswell in his defense. "You see, Doc, this here bunch of Irishmen descended . . ." He paused, glancing suspiciously around at the milling band. "Your musicians . . . I just now noticed. They's all nearly seven feet tall, and youthful. That's not the composition of your typical New Orleans and vicinity marching band."

"Nothing odd about it, though," said Hildy, "when you consider they're actually an elite unit of the Louisiana Private Commandos."

Lasswell quivered. "First Irishmen, now commandos. Why for you bringing commandos into this here crematorium, Doc?"

"Mostly because I'm not Doc," replied Steranko the Siphoner. He meant to remove his false whiskers with a dramatic sweep on his hand but the overly strong glue prevented him.

". . . actual that weren't the really very first time," the glassy-eyed Two-Ton was reciting. "The honest to true first time was in the back seat of my stepdaddy's skycar when I was a cute little feller of twelve and weighed not more than 180 pounds in the buff. Cuddly was how my mom used to describe me. Course she didn't know her cuddly offspring was getting his rocks off with—"

"This can't be what you're after," the impatient blues singer told Jake.

Jake gave the sandwichbox a smack on the side. "The way I rewired this thing, it should be producing a truth beam at this particular setting."

"It is," said Quebec from the sofa next to the sprawled Two-Ton. "He's telling you nothing but the truth. I know, cause I've heard a lot of this before. You got him too far back in the past."

"Can't seem to get him to zero in on Patchwork and the disposal of Shocker Fulson's body."

"*Doctor* Patchwork," said the stupefied Two-Ton. "Dr. Patchwork must be a bright feller . . . leastwise from the hints I overheard . . . Her name was Beulah Lou and I got to tell you she had a pair of knockers on her which—"

"Forget Beulah Lou," urged Jake. "Get back to Dr. Patchwork. Who is he? Where is he?"

"Lot of dough . . . Dr. Patchwork must have a lot of dough . . . heard them boys talking . . . didn't know I was there . . . collecting bodies of all the best crooks around . . . don't make no never mind if they been dead even a couple years or more . . . Didn't wear no lingerie at all . . . first time I stumbled onto that fact it surely give me a thrill . . . unwrapping them is always half the fun . . . Drop the body out over that stretch of no place . . . What's Dr. Patchwork really up to? . . . such a little bitty girl she was, not more than five feet high, but what a set of—"

Thubunk!

Quebec stared up at the ceiling, then at the corridor beyond the half-open door. "What was that?"

Nearsighted Red tapped his lean fingers on the guitar. "This is an odd suggestion to put forth, but I do believe that's the sound a tuba makes when it's dropped to the floor."

Karumb!

"And that there's a trombone being thrown against a wall," Red added.

"Something doing upstairs, Jake." The girl left the sofa. "Could mean more trouble for us."

"We'll depart," he decided, "but I want to take this guy along."

"Cripes," said Red. "What kind of quicky escape we gone bring off lugging that guy?"

"I think he knows more about Dr. Patchwork. I want to find out more about Dr. Patchwork. Ergo, we haul him."

Trump! Katrump!

Trump!

"People coming down the ramp," warned Quebec from the doorway. "Get set for a fight."

Jake straightened up and away from Two-Ton. "Wait now. I recognize one of those sets of footfalls." He went to the corridor and looked out.

"We're coming to rescue you," announced his redhaired wife. Marching down the ramp behind her were six of the members of the spurious Yreka Brass Band.

"Late," said Jake, "as usual."

Chapter 13

————◆————

"This isn't a sulk," said Hildy in a slow precise way. She was sitting as far across the wide floating bed from Jake as she could.

"Oh, so?"

"Because if I were sulking you'd be flat on your kazoo on the floor of this alleged suite," she carefully explained. "When I really work into a good sulk, Jacob, I rehearse in my mind all the injustices which our stormy marriage has caused to be visited upon me. I then come to the inevitable conclusion you are the ultimate source of them all and I'm compelled to give you a good clout in the puss. So this isn't a sulk, though it's edging dangerously close to being."

"Whenever you refer to me as Jacob, that's a prime sulk symptom."

"That is your legal first name, is it not?" Hildy was fully clothed, sitting upright with arms folded. "Jake is merely a boyish nickname, one which you ought seriously to consider shedding at your age. You are after all, Jacob, perilously close to middle age."

"I intend to live to be at least 90. Therefore 45 or thereabouts will be my midlife point."

"Fat chance." She snorted, less politely than usual. "Taking the needless risks you do, cavorting with teenage concubines, sitting in with tacky jazz robots, getting yourself stunned. You'll be lucky to make it to 45, let alone 90."

"In which case 22 was my middle spot and I'm long beyond it and don't have to worry," said Jake. "Speaking, by the way, of screwing up on a mission. How much did those commandos cost?"

"No business of yours."

"We're, as you are fond of reminding, *equal* partners in Odd Jobs, Inc. So I want to know what your foolishness cost my half of the business."

"Saving your life is foolishness, huh? Yes, I suppose it is."

"You could have done that with two commandos, not nine."

"A jazz buff such as yourself, Jacob, ought to know you can't have much of a marching band with only two players."

"You didn't need a marching band at all."

"Your opinion, not mine. You're simply not audacious enough anymore."

"Sitting around on your bare butt . . . is that audacious?"

"Which instance are you alluding to?"

"The most recent obviously, your Swiss violin playing escapade."

"That got results."

"New to me, I haven't heard of any."

"You've been too busy, ever since we turned Boody Lasswell and Two-Ton over to those agents Gunther sent down, criticizing me to listen. Some one on such a tight schedule as you, I wonder you have any time for your wife at all."

"Ah," said Jake. "I see it all at last. You're angry because when you came barging in with those tone deaf black commandos I made some obviously good-natured whimsical remark about your being late. The idea being I'd already managed, as I usually do, to get myself out of trouble."

"A joke which requires an explanation is no joke."

"Didn't I pose as a standup comic during our investigation of the Druid movement in Nebraska last Thanksgiving? Got a hell of a lot of laughs for an unfunny person."

"They'll laugh at anything in Nebraska. Why don't you pop down to Omaha and try them with, 'late as usual'? After I, singlehanded, fight my way out of a madhouse, hypnotize Wildcat Brasher, borrow a skycar registered to—"

"Wildcat was in Switzerland? You never told me that."

"I'm not as fearful of Wildcat as you seem to be. Handling him is a relatively trivial matt—"

"What'd he do to you?"

"Nothing much, Jacob."

"What?"

"Oh, he jumped on me from above, nearly strangled me, administered a knockout drug, wrapped me in a wisecracking straight jacket and left me in a madhouse with a bunch of allegedly goofy artists and writers."

"I'll have to fix him."

"Do you have time?"

Jake said, "Okay, listen, Hildy, you really have to learn how to—"

Pop!

It was time for another confetti shower. Bright colored bits of plaz and faxpaper began to drift down from the ceiling outlets.

"Does that happen often?" Hildy asked.

"Every 15 minutes."

"Makes you look quite festive." She scooped a handful of the bright stuff off the bed top, leaned over and sprinkled it over her husband's head.

Jake caught her wrist, pulled her close to him. "Let's negotiate a truce."

"I'm neutral in this. You're the aggressor."

"Whoa now, Hildy, it was you who . . ." He stopped talking, appeared to be counting off numbers inside his head. "You're probably right. It wasn't a good time to kid you."

"It really wasn't, Jake. I'd been worrying about you ever since I arrived here in New Orleans and discovered you were missing."

"We're back together, we can go to work on the case," he said. "In awhile."

"In awhile," Hildy agreed. "I like you again, Jake. I'm 'gonna give ya a big bouquet of red, red rose' first chance I get."

"Red, red roses!" Jake sat up. "That's what I've been trying to remember." He disengaged himself from his redhaired wife, left the bed. "We have to see Steranko again."

"Can we afford it? You paid him $2000 for information and I gave him another $5000 to assist me in tracking you down, providing commandos and impersonating Doc Inferno, alias the Trojan Horse."

"The acting part he'd have done for free," said Jake. "Right now we have to check over his files on Fancy Dawntreader."

"Too much activity," observed Steranko the Siphoner from his slowly rocking rocker. "That's why you're underweight, Hildy."

"I was thinking the very same thing as I jumped

out of a madhouse window recently," she said. "Me for a sedentary life from now on."

"Heaven help us, both the Paces are masters of the quick comeback."

Jake was leaning against the desk. "How much for the Fancy Dawntreader information?"

"All the wealth of all the fabled kingdoms of the earth couldn't make me look at that elongated bimbo's old gossip shows," said Steranko. "However, for $500 cash I'll reluctantly come to your aid. How does she connect with your investigation?"

"Not sure she does," admitted Jake. "I simply have a hunch I want to follow up."

"Never trust hunches. Facts, recorded and stashed away, are what you have to rely on. Why don't you sit down, Hildy, instead of standing around like an unemployed flagpole."

"Why, thank you, I will." Hildy kneed two vidisc players off the only other chair in the underground fact storehouse and seated herself.

"A little more meat on your bones, you wouldn't be so feisty," said Steranko. "Last time I talked to you two zanies you were planning to investigate that lead we gained from the New Iberia crowd. Isn't that your plan anymore?"

"We'll get to that in the morning," replied Jake. "Seems Shocker Fulson was delivered to an island down in the Gulf of Mexico, name of Escola."

"The Willingham Military College For Girls is there," said the Siphoner.

"The body was delivered to the college, in care of a Colonel Bethune," said Hildy. "With any luck we should know who Dr. Patchwork is by tomorrow afternoon."

"Dr. Patchwork?" Steranko's eyebrows flickered upwards. "You didn't mention him before."

"We don't confide everything in you," said Jake, "despite your fabled trustworthiness."

"Yeah, yeah, spare me the badinage, Jake. Had you mentioned Patchwork earlier I could have helped you out."

"Only recently heard about him. Do you know—"

"Watch." He kicked out at a control toggle.

One of the floating ball TV sets lit up. On its screen a middlesized man with standup hair and an ill-fitting four-piece teachsuit was circling a floating slab, bouncing, hopping, gesticulating. The slab held what appeared to be a recent corpse, partially covered by a candy-striped shroud. ". . . Stumbling blocks even an enlightened station like KHOB-TV outs in the path of progress," the wild-haired man was saying. "Such trouble I had bringing my specimen in here you would not believe. Some fine day, you have my word on it, this creation you see before you will be enshrined in some prestigious narrow-minded institution of so-called higher learning. Yes, with a solid gold plate on its case. The substance of the inscription on that plate will be — Patchwork Man #1A, the Creation of the Most Brilliant & Unsung Man of his Time, Dr. Bascom Wolverton. See how many of you then, my friends, call me Dr. Patchwork behind my back and to my face. See how many so-called eclectic educational channels force me to smuggle my creation into their shoddy studios by pretending it's an item for their ongoing fund-raising auction. No, dear viewers, there's coming a time when my composite people will be recognized for exactly . . ."

"Where and when?" asked Jake. "KHOB is out in San Francisco, isn't it?"

"Good guess," said Steranko the Siphoner as he sedately rocked. "This was aired two and one half years ago out in the Bay City. Represents the good doctor's last television appearance. The Board of Health and the Video Artists Guild bitched so much about him that he was forced off even eclectic stations like KHOB-TV."

". . . for this miracle of science, you well may ask. It is simply this. I, the much-maligned and oft misunderstood Dr. Bascom Wolverton, have unlocked the secrets of nature. Yes, and what you see before you is . . . what?" His crinkly hair quivered as he scowled suddenly off camera. "Didn't I just explain my Patchwork Man was not for auction? How much? $126? Your audience is even more barbaric than I assumed. Now, back to the revelations, my friends. I have succeeded, where all your other school trained biologists and geneticists have failed, in finding the *true* secrets of the genetic code. A cinch for somebody with my native ability. I have gone further, bearding the human brain in its lair. I know what each—yes, I mean *each*—what each cell of the brain is for. Therefore, by utilizing my exclusive process (and it is indeed exclusive even though those idiots in Washington won't grant a patent) for raising the dead, I have been able to create what I call the Patchwork Man. Ah, dear viewers, do you realize, I doubt it, that you are hearing for the first time a name which will someday have an important place in the history of all mankind. The Patchwork Man." He paused in his stalking of the slab to thump the corpse on the chest.

The Patchwork Man sat up. "Mine eyes have

seen the glory of the coming of the Lord," he sang in a beautiful baritone.

Dr. Patchwork nudged the body, causing it to settle down. "The voice of one of our great singers, whose remains his greedy family gladly sold to me. Not that my composite man is merely a source of a splendid singing voice. Ah, no."

Another pat on the chest. The composite man rose up, jumping from the slab and losing his bright shroud. "Piece of cake," he exclaimed in an entirely different voice. He proceeded to lift the heavy slab over his head.

"The abilities of a noted circus strongman have also been . . ."

The screen turned black.

Hildy asked, "Is that all we get for our money?"

"What you saw is all there is. At that point KHOB took Dr. Patchwork from the air. Even in a liberal town like Frisco you can't put naked reanimated corpses on the box."

"Any idea," asked Jake, "where Patchwork is now?"

"Haven't been interested enough to find out. My impression was the guy's a quack, a vaud magician trying to work a new racket."

"If he can really do what he claims, it would explain the murders," said Hildy. "Explain how the killer can look like Faceless Slim and have the MO of Shocker Fulson, among others."

"Yeah, all the killings are the work of one man," added Jake. "A Patchwork Man."

"You two bright lights are always bitching about how money oriented I am. Here I *give* you an important lead toward the solution of your current case and I get not so much as a thank you."

"Thank you," said Hildy.

"Thank you," said Jake. "Now let's see the Fancy Dawntreader stuff."

"With gratitude like this, you can understand why I prefer money." Steranko reached beneath his chair for a switch.

A wall screen went on.

There was the statuesque Fancy, reclining in a seethrough hammock and wearing a one-piece pant suit. ". . . love ya, Raffles Tunny. So we're sending ya a big bouquet of red, red roses . . ."

"Same thing she sent to Sentimental Sid," said Hildy. "But so?"

"Put on the next segment I asked for," Jake requested.

Fancy on a different show, in a different boudoir with a different nightdress. ". . . keep packin 'em in, Busino & Marcus. You got the greatest bawdy comedy act in the Schlock Time Circuit. Here's a big bouquet of roses for ya from your ardent fan . . ."

". . . ya make this hardhearted broad snuffle in her brew with them folksy tunes, Whistlin' Pete Goodwin. Here goes a big bouquet of roses . . ."

"I tell ya, Rance Keane, you're a straight shooter in more ways than one. Which is why the fancy one is sending ya a big bouquet of red, red roses . . ."

"Yeah." Jake stood up. "There's what I was trying to remember."

"She likes to send everybody and his uncle flowers," said Steranko the Siphoner. "Hokey, yes. Sinister, no."

"She doesn't send them the same kind of flowers," Hildy pointed out. "The only ones out of this bunch who got 'red, red roses' were Raffles Tunny and Rance Keane."

"Who happen to be the only two out of the batch who were done in by the Patchwork Man," said Jake.

Steranko snapped his fingers. "She's telling the killer who to smack next."

"We'll go back over all the other victims, see if Fancy sent them red, red roses, too. Then I better warn Sentimental Sid to watch out," said Jake. "I'd say Fancy Dawntreader is deeply involved in the murders."

"Going to break the president's heart," said Hildy.

Chapter 14

The afternoon sky was a clear blue, the Pacific filled in the space between Jake and the horizon with a deeper blue. On the slick rocks below the last surviving seal in California was cavorting. After watching the seal for a moment Jake crossed the patio to the door of the seaside television station.

"Oops, oops, don't fall down, Senator Anmar."

"Strangely woozy . . ."

Coming up behind Jake as he reached for the blue-tinted neoglass door was a bearded man who was helping a thickset older man to stay upright. "Sick?" Jake inquired.

"Never been sick a day in my life," answered the chunky senator, lurching. "The people of California know well . . . Wow! Never seen the old Pacific churn and bounce that way."

The bearded youth winked at Jake. "Truth serum."

Jake held the door open. "Who fed it to him?"

"I did. I'm Honest Buxton. Quite probably you recognize me and are a fan of my KHOB newscast." Honest Buxton guided the tottering senator into the station foyer.

"Can't say I am."

"Mainstream snob? Don't look at the people's vid outlet?"

"Hard to pick up your signal back in Connecticut."

"Better get me into makeup," slurred the wobbly senator.

"Nobody wears makeup on my casts." The bearded newsman plopped Anmar down in a tubchair. "My motto is no bullshit."

The senator wiped his perspiring forehead. "I'm wondering if I was wise to go along with you, Buxton."

"Fear the truth?"

"With this truth serum coursing through me, I may become too honest."

Jake went over to the reception desk where a girl with a sudalap sack over her head and much of her torso was seated in a glass chair. "I'm John Chambers from the Federal Eclectic Broadcasting Agency. We wish to—"

"Take a number chit and wait your turn." Large eyes and a nose had been painted on the sack. Her midriff was bare and her hollow navel had lips painted around it. She gave the impression she was talking out of the decorated navel.

"The FEBA doesn't take a chit and wait," Jake told her in a very official voice. "And how come you appear to be talking out of your stomach?"

"I can see," said the sack-clothed girl, "you government bureaucrats don't keep up with popular entertainment at all."

"Is this part of popular entertainment? Talking through your navel?"

"I happen to be a member of the Bellybuttons. We're a very important Nostalgia Rock group and were it not for a series of unfortunate circumstances we'd be on top of the show-biz heap and I wouldn't be working in this craphole. Take a number and wait your turn."

Jake leaned over her desk, palms pressed out on it, watching her bare stomach area. "You actually control it, make it move like a mouth. How do you do that?"

"Practice," replied the Bellybutton girl.

"I wonder if this is an ability I ought to add to my store," Jake mused. "How do you get the voice to sound like it's coming from down there?"

"Simple ventriloquism."

"That's really—"

"Brace yourselves, everybody!" A rumpled black man had come pushing into the foyer. "There's another one coming!"

Jake inquired, "Another what?"

"Oh," the girl said out of her middle, "that's only Professor Quaker."

Very cautiously the professor made his way to a chair. "I doubt any of us will live until my show goes on. Woops! That was a big mother!"

"He's very sensitive to earth tremors," explained the sacked receptionist. "Claims he can predict earthquakes."

"Wowsie!" Professor Quaker held tight to the arms of his tub. "That was a dandy one. San Fran's likely to go wooshing down into a big hole any minute."

Senator Anmar opened his puffy eyes. "I ought to be with my constituents at a time like this."

Honest Buxton said, "The truth is more important than any earthquake."

Jake returned his attention to the girl. "Could you teach me how to do the contractions?"

"Why? So you can go into competition with us?"

"I'm always anxious to pick up new skills."

"There's something in that. If we don't learn, we stagnate and—"

"Jake! Jake Pace! Exactly the man I want to see!" An inner door had whapped open to reveal a tall blond man in a one-piece white cooksuit.

"This is Mr. Chambers of the—"

"It's Jake Pace. Sure as I'm Barbecue Bob." He hurried across the foyer, took Jake by the arm. "I'm having the devil's own time with my hot sauce, Jake. Was running out to the library to look up a recipe. But you know more about hot sauce than most any man living."

"Gee, he does have eclectic skills," remarked the receptionist, seemingly from her puckered navel.

Jake allowed Barbecue Bob to escort him out of the foyer, down a corridor and into a studio. "You're on the damn air?" Jake asked when he saw the cameras and the kitchen set.

"They're very casual here at KHOB. You can come and go as you like, even during your own show."

When he was out under the lights Jake noticed three people slumped at the kitchen table. The woman in the group was snoring, the two men were groaning with eyes tight shut. A dish of partially eaten spare ribs was sitting in front of each slumped person.

"Volunteers from the audience," explained Barbecue Bob.

Out in the shadows sat some thirty people, including another girl with a sack over her head and torso and a mouth painted around her navel.

"Did your sauce knock them over?" Jack asked.

"Afraid so." Barbecue Bob smiled into a television camera, but not the one which was filming him at the moment. "Hi, audience, I'm back. Look who I was able to bring with me. America's best amateur chef, Jake Pace."

About five people in the studio audience, including the other navel girl, gasped and said, "Ah!"

"Jake is probably better known to you as one of our leading gentlemen adventurers, the co-owner of the famous Odd Jobs, Inc.," continued the cook show host. "He certainly ought to convince you that simply because a man is interested in cooking he isn't a fairy. Right, Jake?"

"In most cases." He was bending over the snoring woman. "This one's having an allergic reaction." He moved around to one of the groaning men. "This guy . . . better get out some baking soda, Bob."

"Leave them be for now, Jake. I admit today's recipe for hot sauce didn't turn out quite right. I was aware of that even before these folks started falling over."

Jake was examining the third hot sauce taster. "This guy's going to need a stomach pump." He sniffed at the plate of ribs. "You used too much wild sage in this."

"Maybe I did," admitted Barbecue Bob. "I'm pretty much a spontaneous cook, as my many viewers know. Never had such dire results before, though. Over at the Top of the Bridge where I'm Master Chef I—"

"You're cooking at the Top of the Bridge now." Jake lifted the most seriously ill audience participant from his chair, laid him out on the studio floor. A camera rolled in for a close shot of the moaning man.

"Been there since last year, Jake. You ought to drop in for a meal on the house. And we've got Sentimental Sid playing nightly."

"I know." Jake had come to San Francisco to keep the Patchwork forces from doing in Sentimental Sid. He'd tried to warn the ballad singer by pixphone, but was rebuffed by one of the singer's private secretaries. So he'd flown out, while Hildy journeyed to the Willingham Military College. Jake wanted, before going up against Sentimental Sid in person, to see if KHOB had anything in their files on the elusive Dr. Patchwork.

"Nix, nix," someone was frantically whispering from the edge of the set. It was a small young man with curly blue hair. "Don't go pumping that guy's stomach on camera."

"Okay, then get him off to a hospital quick," countered Jake.

"Soon as we cut to a closeup of Bob. Come on, one of you guys cut."

When the second camera was concentrating on Barbecue Bob two hunched men ran in to drag the moaning man away.

Jake, grinning his bleak grin, joined the chef. "I'll drop in on you tonight," he said in a low voice. Turning to the camera he raised his voice. "Folks, I'm going to show you how to whip up a tasty hot sauce right now. It's similar to the one which won me a blue ribbon in no less a place than Paris."

"Ah!" exclaimed the studio audience.

Chapter 15

One came at her from the left, snarling. Another bristling black guard dog rushed Hildy from out of the twilight mist at her right. A third dog, a cyborg judging from its heavy rattling gallop, charged directly at her from the front.

"Shoo," she suggested to the trio of big angry dogs as she set her suitcase down on the gravel pathway which wound up from the beach.

The dogs kept coming.

Without warning Hildy dropped flat on her back.

The dogs charging from left and right collided with each other and not with her.

"Cyborgs, too," Hildy decided, judging from the metallic clang the dogs produced on hitting. She made this decision while elbowing across the gravel.

The third dog halted a few yards from her, legs wide, nape hair erect, fangs dripping frothy saliva.

"They overdid that drool when they augmented you, boy." She went rolling away just as the dog made his leap for her.

Springing swiftly to her feet she dealt the partially metallic animal a chopping blow to the throat. "Ouch!"

What would Jake say if he saw her pull something like that? She'd misjudged, applied the paralyzing blow to a metal plate set in the guard animal's neck instead of to its real flesh.

Whirling, paws sending up streams of dust and grit, the dog came for her again.

More observant this time, Hildy dodged the hurtling animal and got in several nice chopping blows.

The dog yelped once, thudded to a limp landing and lay still.

The other two cyborg watchdogs were stumbling around in the misty dusk, feebly snarling and striving to clear their heads.

"Hey, that's great! How'd you manage to do that to Snarly?"

Hildy collected her suitcase, eyes on the wobbling pair of dogs. "You part of the establishment?"

A slim girl, fifteen at the most, stepped out of the swirling mist. The fog made her short-cropped blonde hair sparkle, beaded the brass buttons on her fashion-style two-piece black uniform. "Well, more or less. I am a cadet here at Willingham Military College. My name is Pam Hocky. Who are you?"

Hildy answered, "Miss Coppersmith, the new fencing master."

Pam's eyes widened. "What about Captain LeBlanc? You mean you're replacing her? That's grand."

Hildy started walking up the path and away from the stunned dogs. "All I know is I was sent here by the Firepower Employment Service, which specializes in military college staff placements. They got me my last job over in Cuban Angola. I taught undergrad Terrorism at the Catholic Kibbutz."

"You must lead a great life," said Pam. "I plan to

do the same thing myself. Soon as I'm sixteen I can do as I wish and I'm going to roam and have adventures. You see, I'm a private investigator at heart."

"A detective?"

"Right you are, Miss Coppersmith. Thus far my investigations have been limited to uncovering scandals and corruptions at schools," the blonde young girl explained. "Which is why I've attended eleven different schools so far in my life."

"It does sound adventurous."

"I think so, too, though my parents differ. They're, being electronic evangelists, very conservative. Perhaps you've seen their show. The Rev Brimstone Hocky & Saintly Sister Pearl Video Salvation Experience."

"I think it's on opposite Fancy Dawntreader."

"Oh, her. Do you like her?"

The fog was thickening, had walled the two of them in from everything else. "If you want to keep up with show business, you have to watch her."

Pam lowered her voice. "I can tell you something about Fancy Dawntreader almost no one else at Willingham knows," she said. "Even though you're on the staff side, Miss Coppersmith, I can sense you're someone I can confide in. Being a private investigator I'm very good at making character judgments." The girl's tongue puffed out her cheek for a few seconds. "In fact, my detective instincts tell me you may not be a real teacher at all, but rather some sort of secret operative."

Hildy watched the young girl's face. "You're very perceptive, Pam. I am a secret operative and I'm anxious to find out what you know about Fancy Dawntreader."

Pam slowed. "You're not trying to humor me, the way some . . . No, I don't think you are," she said. "You know, I had an enormous urge to come roaming down to the beach this afternoon. Not that I don't wander off by myself a good deal anyway. Being a private investigator, as you may have noticed, is a lonely life."

"Gets better as you grow older, as do most things." Hildy spotted a wrought-iron bench by the side of the climbing path. "We'll stop over there so you can tell me about Fancy."

"She was here on this island," said Pam when they were side by side on the chill metal bench. "Fancy Dawntreader visited Willingham roughly seven months ago. I have the exact date in my journal, except consulting it is going to be a little tough since I recently concluded burial of the book was the only way to keep it from being got at by the staff. Anyway, I know it was about seven months in the past because I'd just transferred here from the Tibetan Buddhist School of Design out in Berkeley."

"No one else noticed her visit?"

"Only a few, because it was a secret. Fancy Dawntreader arrived one midnight and departed the following sunrise," the girl told Hildy. "This wasn't one of your usual celeb-visits-the-kiddies affairs. No, Fancy sneaked in and out and went only to the old shutdown Life Science Building, in the company of Colonel Bethune and Captain Le-Blanc."

"How'd you happen to witness the visit?"

"As I told you, I roam a lot," replied Pam. "Despite the guard dogs and all, Willingham isn't all that secure. The dorm locks and guard 'bots aren't much challenge to someone with my experience."

"Did you learn what Fancy's visit was all about?"

Pam nodded slowly. "This part of my investigation puzzles me, Miss Coppersmith. My initial impression was I was witnessing some sort of funeral. They went into the LSB, then up to the Second Level to view a body. It was the body of a man, I didn't get a thorough glimpse of him since I was clinging to some decorative vines on the building side at the time."

"Do you know what happened to the body?"

"Well, Snarly and the other dogs had my scent and I had to evade them and hustle back into my dorm," said Pam. "When I had the chance to return to the scene, not for two days because I had a Tank Warfare exam to study for, there was no dead man and no trace of one. Does any of this—"

"Cadet Hocky, why are you sitting down?"

"At the invitation of our new instructor, Lt. Badjett."

A thin young woman of twenty-six had emerged from the fog. Her uniform was more elaborate than the cadet's, and a stungun hung from her broad belt. "New instructor?"

"Jessica Coppersmith at your service." Hildy hopped to her feet, clicked her heels and performed a crisp salute. "Sent to Escola Island by Firepower."

"There's nothing in the dayplan about a new arrival." Lt. Badjett came closer to Hildy, scrutinizing her. "What topic is it you claim to be teaching?"

"Fencing, of course."

"Unlikely. Captain LeBlanc is still hale and hearty. Cadet Hocky, there is no further need for you to attend this conversation.

"Yes, lieutenant." With a lazy salute Pam backed

away from the bench. "See you again, Miss Coppersmith."

"Certainly," smiled Hildy.

"We don't encourage smiling at the cadets, Coppersmith. Do you have any proof of your assertions?"

"A letter from Firepower instructing me to report here this afternoon." Hildy tapped her suitcase with a booted toe. "I must say I'm not impressed with the welcome provided me. Several nasty cyborg dogs attacked me the moment I left the dock and—"

"Coppersmith, there's obviously been some kind of civilian foulup back on the mainland," cut in Lt. Badjett. "If you'll accompany me to Colonel Bethune's office we'll attempt to clear this matter up quickly."

"I'd like that," said Hildy.

The tapping at her cottage door came a few minutes shy of midnight. Hildy had been at the window of the guest cottage the commander of Willingham had reluctantly provided her. She was to be taken off the island in the morning.

Hildy was planning, in another few minutes, to prowl the college grounds, paying special attention to the shut-down Life Science Building.

The tapping was repeated.

"Yes?" she said toward the door. She crossed the parlor, deactivated the lock system and opened the door.

Fog and a glimpse of Pam Hocky greeted her. "They've got another one," the blonde girl announced.

"Come on in."

Pam wore a plyo greatcoat over her uniform.

"Sorry to hear they aren't hiring you, Miss Coppersmith," she said. "But then I don't think you had any real expectation of working here. My conclusions are that you—"

"They've got another what?"

Pam brightened. "Body. They've got another body. A corpse arrived after lights out, two hours ago," she said, glancing all around the parlor. "Do you, by the way, think it's safe to talk in here?"

"No bugs. I went over the whole cottage," said Hildy. "Is Fancy here, too?"

"Not as yet."

"Can you describe the body?"

"A male, black. He's in his late twenties I'd estimate," replied the girl, shedding her greatcoat and tossing it on the floor near a lightstrip pole lamp. "The truly odd thing about him is he seems to have a third eye, right here." She tapped the center of her high forehead. "All three eyes are wide open and staring, which is how I was able to notice them without being close up to the body. Never, in any of my prior investigations, have I come across—"

"X-Ray Brown," concluded Hildy. "He was executed in Nevada three days ago under the Annoying Criminals Act of 1998."

"I don't believe I've heard of X-Ray Brown, and I really try to keep up with all the better known criminals."

"Brown was a mutant, the government kept his career relatively quiet," said Hildy. "His father was an Air Army radarman in Alaska and his mother worked in a microwave sandwichbox plant in Buffalo at the time of X-Ray's birth. So his genetic code got botched and he was born with that third eye and the ability to see through stone and metal. He went into a life of crime at the age of eleven."

"And they executed him?"

"The Annoying Criminal Act provides that if ten or more federal or local law officers sign a petition stating a certain crook gives them all a pain, he can be destroyed as a nuisance."

"Sounds unjust."

"Killing anybody usually is." Hildy picked up her all-season parka from a floating bentwood chair. "I'd like to view that body."

"I'll guide you over to—"

"Nope, you scoot on back to your dorm. I know where that LSB is."

"I don't see any reason why I can't—"

The new knocking on the cottage door was loud.

The knocker didn't wait for an invitation, but shoved into the room. She was a large woman in full uniform. She had a broad, scar-hatched face and carried a saber. "You should have worried about an *outside* bug," the large captain said. "We've been in the watermelon patch listening to you with a soundgun for the past three hours."

Hildy observed, "Must be clammy in a watermelon patch at this hour of the night."

The saber sliced at the air between Hildy and the chunky woman. "I am Captain LeBlanc and I'm here to make certain neither of you live."

Chapter 16

Dusk found Jake traveling over the San Francisco Marina in his rented skycar. Boat and bistro lights were blossoming 1000 feet below.

The small box he'd attached to the control panel started beeping.

Without looking up through the neoglass cabin lid, Jake reached down and changed his shoes. Then he grabbed a knapsack off the empty passenger seat and attached it to his back.

"Going to force you down, old buddy." A hearty voice came chuckling out of his comsystem. "Make it easy, or make it rough."

"Wildcat himself." Jake glanced over his shoulder.

The Federal Police agent's white and blue skycar was above and behind him in the deepening twilight.

"Not that I wouldn't enjoy a good old-fashion dogfight," intruded Wildcat Brasher's voice.

Jake leaned very slightly forward, making several adjustments to the controls.

All at once his ship began an arcing climb. When it had executed exactly one half of a perfect Immelmann loop and was passing upside down over Wildcat's skycar, Jake unhooked his safety gear and flipped the lidpopper.

He went plummeting straight out of his car, heading for the other ship.

As he fell Jake executed a swift somersault. He hit the rear fuselage of Wildcat's skycar upright and flatfooted. The sucshoes he'd slipped into held him fast.

From out his knapsack he tugged a glassgutting gun.

Before Wildcat was through disengaging himself from the drive seat Jake was sharing the cabin with him.

"Showoff stunt," rumbled the big FP. "But it won't . . . oof!"

The backpack also held a stungun of Jake's own design. He'd extracted it, used it on Wildcat.

As the big man stumbled, knelt and thumped over, Jake lunged and put the wobbling skycar on an automatic fly pattern. His own car, set before he'd departed it, was tailing this one.

They were out over the Alcatraz Island resort area now, with the Golden Gate Bridge on their left. Jake could see the neoglass walls of the Top of the Bridge restaurant glowing pale orange.

"What brings you to Frisco?" He slapped a truth bug against Wildcat's skull.

The little metal disc took root and the agent was compelled to respond. "Same thing brought you, chum. I got wind Sentimental Sid was the next to get it."

Jake had put the skycars on a circle pattern. They were at the closest point to the bridge restaurant now. "Tonight?"

"Probably. I'm going there now to powwow with Sid," said the mind-controlled federal agent. "Going to stash you in limbo until I get this mess cleared up. Wildcat Brasher's going to be the first to crack this case."

"How'd you get the lead to Sentimental Sid?"

"Boy, it gives me a royal pain in the butt to have to confide in you this way, Pace," he said. "Anyhow, your smart wife missed a couple clues in the land of the Swiss. I didn't. I found out how the Patchwork Man was transported to Raffles Tunny's vicinity and how he got away again. That led me back to the USA, to a flunky who happened to know a few things his bosses didn't think he was wise to. From him I went to a clunk in Memphis. A little dedicated application of the old mitts and an electrostick got me some juicy info."

"Do you know who Dr. Patchwork is?"

"Sure, he's a nutty pecker named Dr. Bascom Wolverton."

"Where is he?" Jake hadn't been able to get any location information from the KHOB people.

"That I don't know. But when this Patchwork bastard shows to knock off Sid, your Wildcat buddy's going to trail him right to Dr. Patchwork's hidey hole. You can bet your buns on that."

"What about motive?"

"Same as always, loyalty to this damn fine land we—"

"Not your motive, dimwit, Dr. Patchwork's."

"He wants to control show biz, that's got to be the motive. After a certain amount of terror, he's going to make his pitch."

"Any other leads?"

Wildcat groaned. "Sheesh, I truly hate spilling my beans to you, but what else can a guy do with a frapping parasite on his coco," he said with a snarl. "My Memphis contact mentioned the Shrine down in Monterey, California, as being tied in with this somehow. Haven't had a chance to crash it yet."

"That's right down the coast from here. What's there?"

"Some kind of way station maybe. Like I said I—"

Kablam! Slam!

An enormous explosion nearby jiggled the skycar, tossing it high and then low.

One entire viewall of the bridge restaurant had come shattering out into the new night.

"Vincent 'Human Bomb' Pasko," said Jake with an angry shake of his head.

"Huh? I don't think so clear with this thing burrowing in my skull. What do you mean?"

"I mean while we've been gabbing out here the damned Patchwork Man has used the abilities of the late Human Bomb to get rid of Sentimental Sid."

"He looked like that guy . . . what's his name? . . . used to be president or something . . . Abe Lincoln," said the black waiter.

"Faceless Slim," muttered Jake.

"There was never a president named Faceless Slim, was there?" The waiter looked from Jake to the two San Francisco Territory lawmen who shared the glass-walled restaurant office with him.

"Jake Pace is giving us the benefit of his vast knowledge of crime and criminals," remarked Murder-Lt. Tudor, a grim, gaunt man.

"Extra knowledge," put in Murder-Sgt. Huang, "is often like fabled butcher's thumb of old. Can tip balance."

Tudor scowled at his partner. "What did I tell

you about the epigrams, Luc? Quit with that
stuff."

"Habit like chains binding Prometheus to mountain, hard to break."

"Quit, just quit now."

"Do you guys wish my eye-witness account or
not?" inquired the waiter.

"Yeah, continue."

Jake eased out of the office of the Top of the
Bridge, wandered into the now customerless room
where Sentimental Sid had been blown to frag-
ments by a wave of the Patchwork Man's hand
while in the middle of *My Mother's Eyes*. Three
Morgue Squad andies were still gathering up remains with rotoscoops while a perspiring Lt.
Coroner stood by trying not to watch.

"I envy you, Jake," the young coroner called.
"You've found a way to make a darn good living
from this dreadful business."

"You'll never get anywhere on salary, Leviton.
Go freelance."

"Tough to find work as a freelance coroner."

Jake continued on to the kitchen area of the
restaurant which was built smack in the middle of
the Golden Gate Bridge. In the parking area outside this kitchen he'd landed both the skycars, leaving Wildcat in one with the control disc
incapacitating him.

"Hardly a time to talk about food, Jake," said
Barbecue Bob. "I did, though, want to bum another
recipe off you. My Coquilles St. Jacques didn't go
over tonight. What would you suggest for—"

"Go easy on the bay leaf, that's the secret."

"About eight customers keeled over from the
stuff, but the explosion made most everybody forget about it. Lucky."

Jake surveyed the vast opaque-walled room. Barbecue Bob was the only human employee in it. "Witnesses say the killer ran in here after pointing at Sid."

"How did the guy kill poor Sid? Merely with a gesture? I've never heard of—"

"It's a wild talent a few people have, a variation on the telekinetic gift," Jake explained rapidly. "You told the cops you didn't see anyone come in here after the explosion?"

"What I told Murder-Lt. Tudor and his aphoristic little partner was not strictly true, I guess," said the chef. "I mean I did see somebody, but not the killer. The lieutenant—and he strikes me as a chap who doesn't enjoy his food—wanted to know if I'd seen a man with an uncanny resemblance to Abe Lincoln, onetime president of the United States. I honestly replied no. The only person I saw was the moon-faced young fellow from AndyRep over in Marin."

"There was a repair man here at the time of the killing?"

"We'd been having trouble with one of the Gypsies in the washroom," amplified Barbecue Bob. "Instead of playing Romany airs this android's been getting off hoedown tunes. Not at all right for the john."

"Did this AndyRep guy have IDs?"

"Possibly he did. We were expecting a repair man, a repair man knocked at the door. Besides, my Coquille people were starting to fall over about the time the fellow arri—"

"Faceless Slim can mold his face into any shape, though he frequently leaves it blank." Jake crossed to the back exit. "Know how the guy arrived?"

"Ask Herky, our landing attendant."

Jake had the door open. "Landing attendant? There's nobody out here."

"There has to be, Jake. Herky, being an android, is always there." He came trotting after Jake. "He never takes a snycaf break or goes to the biffly."

Jake was out on the bridge-wide sycar landing lot. The night was relatively clear, the stars hardly hazy. Jake dropped down, stretched out flat on the speckled surfacing. "I hear something . . . yeah, it's an andy's motor running."

"Nobody can hear an android's motor," said the puzzled chef.

"Some makes you can, if you know how to listen." Up on his feet again, Jake went sprinting to the bridge rail. "Hecky's underneath here someplace." He gripped an orange-painted cable, swung over the rail and climbed under the landing lot. "Yeah, here he is."

Barbecue Bob, careful not to stare down, came to the rail. "What's he doing under there?" he called.

"Somebody magnetized him and stuck him to the underside out of the way." Jake fetched the demagnetized Herky, who'd been pressed against the metal bridge. With a one-handed thrust he got the attendant up onto the bridge cables. "Climb over to the lot," he instructed the now-functioning mechanism.

"Tsk tsk," observed Herky as he did as he was told. "What an experience."

"What were you doing under there, Herky?" Barbecue Bob asked as the android and Jake hit the topside lot.

"I have only my insatiable curiosity to blame, sir." Herky dusted off his one-piece coverall. "I took to wondering why AndyRep didn't send their usual man, and was so bold as to ask the fellow who professed to—"

"Was that when he arrived?" asked Jake.

"Right you are, sir. The fellow magnetized me with but a touch of his hand before I got hardly a question out. Then, using impressive strength, slipped me down under."

"Shocker Fulson could do that magnetizing trick," mused Jake.

Barbecue Bob said, "I thought the killer's name was Faceless Slim."

Jake ignored him, concentrating on the android. "What kind of skycar was he using?"

"A dark green Nolag, last year's model," replied the attendant. "Which is another thing which put me on the wonder. There was, to be sure, the usual AndyRep sticker on the door, but the car was much fancier than they usually give their repair persons."

"Which direction did it come from?"

Herky pointed toward Marin County, across the Bay from San Francisco. "I'd estimate, from its arrival path, the skycar came from Sausalito. There are a goodly amount of robots and androids over in the Gaytown Sector, so it's—"

"Thanks." Jake ran to his own skycar. "Don't forget, Bob, easy on the bay leaf." In less than a minute he was in the air and aimed for Sausalito. "It's possible the Patchwork Man headed back to Sausalito after doing in Sentimental Sid."

"You'll never find out, buddy boy." Wildcat rose up from beneath a backseat thermal laprobe. A stunrod was clutched in his beefy fist.

Chapter 17

———◆———

Gritting her teeth, Captain LeBlanc thrust the saber straight at Hildy's middle. "We don't like snoops!"

Hildy pivoted, spun out of the way of the charging instructor.

"You're certainly not displaying the kind of sportsmanship," said Pam as she flattened back against a wall of the cottage parlor, "you stress in class, captain."

"The lamp there," Hildy said to the young girl. "Toss it."

"At her?"

"To me."

"Now for the fatal slash!" Chunky Captain LeBlanc had recovered from her collision with a floating bookbin and was again charging the unarmed Hildy.

Catching the pole lamp two handed, Hildy shoved the rod to meet the downcoming slice of the sword.

Clang!

The vibrations caused the captain's arm to quiver. "A saber can both cut and thrust," she said through slightly chattering teeth. She attempted a thrust under the defending lamp.

Hildy brought the floor lamp straight down. The

rod again hit the blade and kept it from touching her body.

Klung!

"A temporary setback, but . . . ow!"

Hildy swung the light strip end of the lamp up to connect with the captain's several chins. Letting go of the improvised weapon, she spun aside and booted her now-staggering opponent in the rump.

Captain LeBlanc enacted a hunched over gallop into the nearest wall. After a thunking stop against the neoplaster, her breath came whooping out of her.

Hildy sailed over a divan, caught the captain by her uniform collar. She yanked her upright, smacked her three times in the jaw and allowed her to decline to the cottage floor.

"You have a very unconventional style of combat." Pam moved gingerly closer. "Effective, though."

Hildy gathered up the captain's saber, strode to the still open doorway and tossed it out into the night. "We'll get rid of—"

"Yike! Owchie! Unk!" someone cried out there among the trees.

"Captain LeBlanc had a backup," said Hildy, frowning at darkness. "Sounds like the sword nicked her."

"Very deft," Pam said admiringly.

Hildy said, "I'm going over to the Life Science Building. They seem to have the wind up so—"

"I'll have to tag along. Since they know I'm assisting you, Willingham Military College For Girls isn't going to be very safe for me."

"Sorry," said Hildy, stooping to pick up her suitcase. "I seem to have dealt another blow to your academic career."

"Think nothing of it, I was getting really tired of all this. Let's go."

After a few seconds' hesitation, Hildy stepped out into the night. "We'll move carefully, Pam. We don't know how many troops are out tonight."

"Did you kill the person you speared with the saber?"

"No, only wounded. She went limping off back for the main buildings."

"How do you know that?"

"Heard her, while we were talking."

Pam shook her head as she followed Hildy into the surrounding woods. "I thought I had keen ears, being a private investigator, but you—"

"We'll practice a little woodland silence," instructed Hildy.

A green throbbing.

Screams of pleasure, electric music. Amplified voices booming.

Jake sat up.

That was a mistake. Strange pains went zigzagging from his head down his spine.

The night sky was partly masked by leaves and branches.

"Still plenty of places on the racks, lads!" an amplified voice was invitingly chanting downhill somewhere. "A few choice whipping posts to be had!"

"Blung," said Jake, it being the only word he found himself capable of uttering.

He touched his head near the spot where Wildcat had bopped him with a pistol handle. An enormous lump, but no skin broken.

"Subtle," said Jake. That was better, a real word.

"That bastard is certainly subtle, banging me over the head with a gun."

"Sadists! Here's your chance! Several choice whips and scourges available!" another voice drifted up from the greenlit business district below the forest Jake had awakened in.

He arose, assuming a position that would have conveyed lack of confidence in his equilibrium to any witness. "Underestimated Wildcat," Jake admitted. "Stupid bastard managed to get that parasite off his thick neck, eavesdropped on my interview with Herky and snuck himself into my skycar. Not bad work for a lout."

"Lovely boys in classic bondage poses! Come in and gape!"

Jake's zigzag pains weren't knifing so thoroughly through him. He straightened up completely. "Dumped out of my own skycar. Dumped on the outskirts of Gaytown. Ah, the ignominy of it all."

He worked his way out of the woods and rented a landcar from the lot of Bisex Billy.

Chapter 18

On his left a floating roadsign announced *Beach-bums Shrine This Exit!* Jake swung his landcar off the see-through ramp which had been carrying him along the coast high above the bright Pacific. Before he reached dry ground the buildings started talking to him.

". . . only authorized relics! Get 'em at Mother Malley's Sanctified Boutique and . . ."

". . . whatever you want in our completely soundproof suites! For the rest of your life, it's got to be the Blessed Virgin Skytel and . . ."

". . . 48 Golden Hits by the only rock group ever canonized by the church! Yes, you get four dozen of the immortal Beachbums' big ones on a single audiochip no bigger than your nostril. Yes, you get *Slurpin' In the Surf, Surfin' Slurp, Slurpy Surf* . . ."

". . . entire miraculous vision seen by California's only saints so far now on six beautifully illuminated Viewmaster discs which you and your family will cherish until . . ."

Jake tried all the blocking toggles on the dash of his rented car, but the intrusion messages kept pouring out of the voxbox, interrupting each other.

". . . lifesize rubberoid images of the beloved Beachbums which lovingly and breathtakingly recreate the very poses they struck when they saw the Virgin Mary rise out of the waters off Pismo Beach on that fateful day back in 1996 while . . ."

". . . only tri-op comic book version of *Our Later Life & Good Works*, the miraculous tome penned by the four Beachbums after they'd witnessed their miracle and renounced their career as America's superhit Surfrock group and turned to a life of contemplation and good . . ."

". . . you act at once you get also the original versions of *Surfin' & Slurpin'*, *Let's Slurp in the Surf*, *Listen To the Surf Go Slurp* . . ."

The stilt buildings which were beaming messages at all the cars turning off the Pacific Seaway were also blinking slogans out into the hot afternoon. Jake tried to ignore all that as he drove into Monterey, California, in search of a place to park.

Blessed Virgin Skydrive Lots 1 and 2 were full. The Sainted Beachbums Panoramic Parking Dome was full, as were Lots 1, 2 and 3 of the Our Lady of Pismo chain.

Jake found a spot finally, some four miles from the actual Shrine in the Used-To-Be-A-School Park-It-Yourself Lot.

"Like to get snarfed on sacred ground?" a pretty fourteen-year-old girl inquired when Jake stepped off the lot. She was dressed merely in a plyoponcho, taking her ease beneath a plastic palm tree.

"I'm in Monterey for sacred rather than profane reasons," he told her.

"Aw, you probably don't even know how to snarf anyhow. I bet you're a poffer."

Jake flashed her an especially evil grin and continued on his way.

"Saint bones! Saint bones! Get 'em whiles they last!" A huge blind Negro was blocking the sidewalk. There was a very large and surly police dog standing at his side and a wicker basket of yellowed bones rattling in his hand. "I got the only true bones of the blessed Beachbums. I can sell you bones from important parts of all four of America's new and favorite saints. I can—"

"No, thanks." Jake started to circle the man and the dog.

"You better buy a bone, Jim," suggested the blind vendor. "Else I have my mean dog bite a hunk out of your fanny."

"Tell your mean dog I'll break his neck if he so much as snarls," grinned Jake.

The vendor swallowed once. "Go with God."

There were three lines of visitors outside the Shrine. Over each of the entrances figures had been painted—$20, $40, $60. The shortest tourist line was at the $60 entrance.

"Might as well go first cabin." Jake put himself in the shortest line.

The Shrine of the Blessed Beachbums had been, in the later decades of the 20th century, the home of the Surfrock quartet. Since their canonization three years earlier the home had been maintained as a shrine, with everything kept exactly as the Beachbums had left it. There was a deflated airfloat mattress on the swayback porch, along with most of an electric motorcycle and half a pair of skis. Empty beer pods and whisky plazflasks were thick on the small yellow lawn. A 1990s style bra dangled from the broken lightstrip fixture over the nibbled doormat.

Immediately to the front of Jake in the $60 line was a middle-aged woman in a tight one-piece funsuit of a sunburst pattern. "I used to love them, just absolutely love them," she confided to him. "I have all their cassettes. Bought them then, kept them always. To buy those cassettes now would cost you thousands of dollars, *if* you could find them. Why did they have to die so young in that alleged bordello explosion? I cried a week when that happened. Well, not a week but six days nonstop. Then I had to go back to work at the fishmeal plant. Your idols may die, yet life goes on. Isn't that right?"

"Whenever any of my idols dies, those are the first words which come to mind." Jake grinned at her.

"You possess, hope you don't mind my mentioning, a malevolent smile." The woman shivered.

"Next six, we can take the next six now. Once inside you'll pay up and wait to be summoned further into the Shrine." A pale man squinted out at them through a partially open doorway. "That will mean up to and including the lady in the sunburst funs . . . um . . . make that the next seven. We can take the next seven, which will be up to and including the tall lean gentleman with the devilish grin. Come inside and wait for your guide."

When they reached the inside, finding themselves in what once had been the Beachbums' washroom, there was no sign of the pale man who'd done the obvious take on noticing Jake.

"Oh, this is their own washer-dryer system," exclaimed the sunburst woman while timidly stroking one of the dented appliances.

Jake worked his way through the half dozen tourists in the narrow room and reached another door.

"Funny nobody took our money yet," remarked a Negro business man to his wife. "Usually they grab that before you been more than ten seconds inside here."

"Don't go making irreligious remarks, Oscar. Just stand and wait, like the man instructed."

Jake opened the door and stepped into the Beachbums' kitchen, closing the door behind him. There was no one in the small yellow and green room. A single horsefly made zoom noises up under a plyocurtain over the dirty sink.

"There's a blaster pointing right at yer liver and lights," a familiar voice informed him from behind. "If you come along, Jake, I'll show ya some things visitors don't get a gander at."

Jake slowly turned. "Ah, one of my idols."

Fancy Dawntreader had stepped out of a pantry closet. The very tall, platinum-haired girl held a blaster pistol. "Ya know, Jake, yer the second big somebody who's dropped in today."

"Build a better shrine and the world'll—"

"We caught that musclebound buffoon Wildcat Brasher at the crack of dawn," amplified the celebrated gossip. "Once he talked, we knew we hadda be on the lookout for ya."

"I suppose Wildcat and I are candidates for bouquets of red, red roses."

"Wildcat we got in a suspended state down inna underground facilities. I ain't sure about you, but for now you come on down there, too. See I—"

"Help! Help!" Jake suddenly shouted. "They're after my relics! Help!"

"Knock off that kinda—"

"Heathens! Infidels!" Jake stomped on the kitchen floor, flapping his arms. "Help!"

The door he'd come through snapped open. Six curious tourists came stumbling into the kitchen.

"Yer supposed to wait out there for yer guide!" Fancy yelled at them. "Can't ya read them signs?"

"Is she really robbing you?" asked the middle-aged funsuited woman.

"She wants the sacred bones I just purchased," Jake told them all.

"Those bones aren't likely to be authentic," said the Negro businessman. "So it's hardly worth a—"

"Go back inna washroom, you schmucks!" Fancy stomped her foot. "This bird is feeding ya a line of crapola."

"I may as well introduce myself." Jake grinned at the tourists. "I'm Special Agent Arnowitz of the Religious Division of the Federal Police and this young woman is the notorious Sophie Lang."

"She does look very familiar," said the woman in the funsuit.

"You've no doubt heard of her string of sacrilegious crimes." Jake walked over to Fancy, slapped the pistol from her hand, pocketed it and gave the startled girl a paralyzing chop to the neck.

The long tall gossip folded. Jake stooped and caught her over his shoulder as she fell. "I'll convey her to our local office now," he said to the group. "Thank you all for your cooperation."

"Does the government now sanction coldcocking a woman?" the Negro asked.

"We're equal now," his wife reminded him. "I got as much right to be coldcocked as you do, Oscar."

Jake carried the unconscious Fancy out of the kitchen and into the hall. Eight more tourists were trailing along behind a pleasant-faced girl who was saying, ". . . the very bed they slept in." She came to a stop, giving Jake a wide-eyed stare. "You oughtn't to be carrying her draped over you like that, sir."

"Take me downstairs at once," he told the girl evenly.

"I have to guide these people to the Beachbums' sanctified bedroom so they may—"

"Ladies and gentlemen," Jake said to this batch of Shrine buffs, "I am Dr. Spurgeon Mamlish, the noted obfuscationist. This unfortunate young woman I am toting must be treated at once. I'm certain none of you will object to this young lady's guiding me down to the firstaid room. No, I thought not." With his recently acquired blaster pistol he gestured at the girl.

"You're going to get it." With a sigh she left the group shuffling in the hallway and headed off toward a blind door. "In here, Pace."

When the girl opened the door to reveal a dark down ramp, Jake said, "You first, little missy."

"You don't think you can long oppose the Ladies Mafia, do you?"

"So that's who I've been tangling with. Splinter group, are you?"

"Much more than that, Pace."

"Downward now," he urged. "Lead on."

The girl waved a hand and light strips came on. "You're never going to be able to—"

"Guide, don't comment."

With another sigh the pleasant-faced girl led Jake down beneath the Shrine.

Chapter 19

"Is this a setback, chief?"

"Will ya keep yer yap shut, Mona," the awake Fancy Dawntreader suggested.

The dumpy brunette in the two-piece white worksuit slid open a panel in the grey wall, tugged out a bodytub. "Here he is, the only non-dead one we've got stored."

Jake viewed the unconscious Wildcat. "Looks very natural," he observed. "What'd you use to knock him out with?"

"Talk about tough," replied Mona. "It took two shots of Stunoleum, which as you may know is a trade name for the generic drug known as—"

"Button yer lip, din I tell ya." Fancy poked her tongue against the back of her teeth, scowling at Jake and the blaster he held. "Don't tell that bird nothing ya don't have to."

"I assumed," said Mona, "the jig was up. Here comes the noted Jake Pace, marching you into one of the secret underground rooms in the until now hidden headquarters of the Ladies Mafia after incapacitating several of our staff. Well, I naturally concluded—"

"Keep yer gloomygus opinions to yerself. Maybe the jig is up an maybe it ain't."

"It's up," Jake assured both women. "Stunoleum

usually keeps a victim out for at least 48 hours . . ."

"We can bring him awake with an injection of Vitazine, the trade name for—"

"We'll allow him to awaken naturally," Jake said. "But heft him out of that tub."

Dumpy Mona stooped to oblige. "One Wildcat coming up."

"Don't bust your fanny for this guy. Let him heft his own pal out."

"Oh, it's no bother, Fancy." Mona inserted a hand under the Federal Police agent's collar and got him entirely out of the bodytub with one powerful tug. "I'll prop him in the corner for now."

"Do that," said Jake. "Have you a supply of Stunoleum and a needlegun?"

"Ya don't think yer gonna stun my entire staff, do ya?"

"Many as I can before I pixphone the Show Biz Department to come gather you up."

"Fat chance ya got of bringing that off, shorty."

Jake grinned up at the 6'7" woman. "Quick, Mona, the Stunoleum." Out of the corner of his eye he watched the dumpy girl reform a vial of the drug and a needlegun from a cabinet. "Stay right over there."

"Darn, how'd you know I was planning a suicide charge of your flank?"

"Instinct. Load the gun. That's right. Now apply it to your arm. Go on, squeeze the trigger."

"I'm a little unnerved at having to—"

"Squeeze."

Mona administered a dose of the knockout drug to herself. In less than a minute her dumpy body was sprawled upon the floor next to the sleeping Wildcat.

"Ya gonna feed me a shot of that stuff?"

"You I need conscious." With a swift motion of his free hand Jake snapped a control bug against the snowy-haired girl's neck. "You'll have to answer anything I ask. First question . . . where's Dr. Patchwork?"

"Take a leak in yer sombrero, ya . . ." Fancy's lovely eyes glazed, her long tall body stiffened slightly. "Nobody knows."

"You don't know where Dr. Patchwork is?"

"Part of the deal I made with him," replied the mind-controlled gossip. "I pay him his fees, he maintains his privacy. When the Ladies Mafia is in more control of the country, then he'll probably come out of the woodwork. He was a pretty frustrated old buzzard before I gave him his chance to shine."

Jake nodded at the walls of the underground room. "You're collecting bodies here, to construct more Patchwork Men apparently. How do you get them to Dr. Patchwork?"

"Once every two weeks, on a prearranged schedule, we leave whatever we got at a prearranged location."

"Where?"

"It's a condemned stretch of beach down beyond Malibu. The bodyboxes are dumped there at midnight, along with any dough I owe the old geezer."

"You don't see him, talk to him?"

"Part of our deal," answered Fancy. "I only had contact with him the few times it took to set up our deal. I'd seen Dr. Bascom Wolverton on the tube couple years back. When I began organizing, working out my plan to get a piece of all the show biz money in the USA, I remembered him. Figured out how he'd fit in with what I had in mind."

"Who's funding all this?"

"Mostly me. I got a terrific contract on my show. And I got to admit the real Mafia's helped out a little, as have some guys who ain't too satisfied with the AM. Naturally they can't hold office in the Ladies Mafia, but I can toss 'em a piece of the pie now and then. Ya know?"

"You use your gossip show to tell the doctor who to hit next," said Jake. "With the 'red, red rose' business. Right?"

"Ya wanna cigar for guessing that?"

"Is that message going out directly to Dr. Patchwork?"

"Yeah, the old bird ain't got no minions. He watches my show every single night."

"And every now and then you tell him who to hit next and where that victim is."

"Ya can't have a terror campaign without bumping off a few schmucks."

"Comparing your past broadcasts with the assassination dates, it works out that Wolverton and the Patchwork Man strike within two days of your message."

"Yeah, two or three days."

Jake asked, "When's your next drop of bodies at Malibu?"

"Twelve days hence. We only just unloaded a pair of stiffs the other day."

"Since his pickup site is in Southern California, his headquarters are likely there, too."

"Lot of goofy people live in Southern Cal. I figure the old buzzard's there, too, except I gave up trying to find out exactly where. Lost three promising Ladies Mafia girls that way. Not one showed up again after I put 'em to tailing him after he showed to pick up the stuff."

"Do you think he goes along with his Patchwork Man on the jobs?"

"My guess is he goes along. He's too protective of his comp to let him out alone. It's, ya know, a parental sort of thing."

"Yeah, so—"

The door of the body-storage chamber suddenly flew open. A blonde young girl pushed a wheeled cart in. Atop the cart rested a neowood coffin. "Hi, sorry we're a little late with X-Ray Brown but we had some engine trouble between here and Escola Island. You may also be wondering what happened to the girl who flew your skyvan back to Willingham to pick up the body and I'd like to explain about that. I'm actually a—"

"Back away from the box," ordered Jake. "Back to the wall."

The young girl licked her lips. Then she tapped on the coffin lid three times. "Armed man," she said from the side of her mouth before she complied with Jake's instructions.

"Who are you—"

"I'll thank you to drop the . . . oh, hello, Jake." The lid of the box flipped off and Hildy sat up with a blaster pistol in each hand aiming at him. "Don't remark on my being late again."

"Is that man your illustrious husband, Mrs. Pace?" asked Pam Hocky from against the wall. "He looks much grimmer than I expected."

"Yes, he strikes most people that way." Hildy swung out of the box. "Not a bad way to get in here, do you think? We left the late X-Ray Brown back on the island with the college personnel we had to stun. Flew out here in their skyvan, after asking them a few pertinent questions, landed in the designated parking lot and traveled through the secret tunnel to this spot."

"Admirable," commented Jake. "You can help me stun some people down here. Then we have to figure out how to net the elusive Dr. Patchwork."

Chapter 20

———————

Jake circled the huge lemon-yellow bed once more, hand stroking chin. "Not too bad I guess."

"Whatcha mean not too bad, chump? The old fancy one looks terrifico. I ain't kidding ya."

Squatting, Jake made a frame of his fingers to study the bed through. He nodded over his shoulder at one of the television cameramen. "How's it look?"

"Convincing, Mr. Pace. And I've worked the Fancy Dawntreader show going on three years."

"Told ya, din I, chowderhead?" said Hildy, who was reclining on the floating circular bed. She wore a peekaboo one-piece pantysuit and a platinum wig.

With a nod, Jake crossed the floor of the Burbank Sector television studio to stand beside Gunther Stool. "What do you think?"

"I buy it," said the jowly Secretary of Show Biz. "Of course, I'm not a regular viewer of Fancy's Focus. It's possible I may be overestimating the effectiveness of Hildy's impersonation."

"We've got to fool Dr. Patchwork."

"I'd like, hopefully, to fool Ramblin' Billy, too."

"Haven't you told the president yet about Fancy Dawntreader and the Ladies Mafia conspiracy?"

"We agreed, when I arrived in Monterey this

morning, to keep Fancy's arrest a secret until this Patchwork fellow was caught," Stool reminded. "To the best of my knowledge, I've been able to do that. Although the president is already quite glum because Fancy's broadcast last evening was a rerun. He's also unhappy he wasn't able to make his usual nightly call to her."

"There's how Fancy Dawntreader came to know a hell of a lot of what she knew about your operations, Gunther. From those nitwit calls of Ramblin' Billy's."

"My intention, Jake, is to break all of this to him after we tie up the loose ends."

Jake strode back onto the set. "More languor, Hildy."

"How's this hit ya?" The disguised Hildy gave a cat-like stretch, settling deeper into the frilly bedding.

"Maybe a touch too much bosom."

"Too much? I'm supposed to be Fancy Dawntreader, ain't I?"

"We're on the air in three minutes, Mr. Pace." A sweet-smelling man in a skyblue suit was at Jake's side. "Say, I've been meaning to mention this since first you entered our little studio. Didn't I see you up in Gaytown the other—"

"All in the line of duty," Jake told the show's director.

"More's the pity. Now if you'll move off the set we'll make our last minute adjustments."

Jake, one knee on the floating bed, leaned close to his wife. "Good luck, be careful."

"Me? I'm not taking any chances," she said in her own voice. "It's you we're setting up as a target."

Absently watching the dark Pacific, Jake shifted the wooden dummy from his left knee to his right. "How can you be so stupid, Corky?"

"Um, it's because I apply myself, Mr. McGinty."

"Lips," said Hildy from a sling chair near the wide-view window of their rented beach house.

"Um, what's the sort of pretty lady talking about, Mr. McGinty?"

"Merely a heckler, Corky."

"Your lips are moving," said Hildy.

"Hildy, you don't appreciate the subtlety of my impersonation," Jake told her as he moved the dummy back to his left knee. "Anybody who's watched the real Preston McGinty & Corky knows McGinty's one ventriloquist whose lips can be seen to move. Now watch this."

"Um, Mr. Pace," the dummy seemed to say, "what do I have to do to get a wife like yours?"

"Well, Corky, you might try breaking a mirror or walking under a ladder or—"

"Your silly lips are moving just as much now, Jake."

"Professional jealousy," Jake told her from his perch on the floating divan.

"Is that a dig about my Fancy Dawntreader act? Gunther informed me I even fooled Ramblin' Billy Dahlman."

"No great achievement."

"Um," asked Corky, "is the president stupid, too?"

"And he didn't even have to work at it."

"That, gosh, sure cheers me up. If I keep applying myself I could maybe get stupid enough to be president, Mr. . . . say, are you Mr. Pace now or Mr. McGinty?"

"Depends on Mrs. Pace's attitude."

Hildy left her chair. "I know why you're putting on this feisty facade."

"I'm simply polishing my ventriloquism. I have to take the real Preston McGinty's place in the Vigorish Vanities tomorrow night, remember?"

"That's exactly why you're feisty, Jake." She came across the wide living room. "I set you up as Dr. Patchwork's next target, by 'sending ya a big bouquet of red, red roses' tonight. Now you're worried, unsettled over—"

"You really think some crackpot in a tacky suit scares me?"

"I don't like your making yourself a decoy." She put her fingertips to the back of his neck.

"Gunther isn't going to be able to keep this whole mess quiet for another two weeks. Once Patchwork learns Fancy and her burgeoning Ladies Mafia have been taken into custody, he'll vanish. Along with his patchwork killer," Jake said, lowering the dummy to the floor. "So we have to get him to move out into the open as soon as possible. Setting Preston McGinty up as the next victim does that. And with me as McGinty there's no danger."

"No danger to McGinty." She lowered herself onto his lap. "Jake, you have to admit Dr. Patchwork's completely crazy by now. I know Fancy passed him a hefty piece of money to help her, but he has to be goofy to use his composite people for murder."

"Typical revenge pattern." Jake moved his palm along her back. "Same sort of thing that motivates snipers and suicide killers like the one Fancy sent after us in Connecticut. Get back at the society which has ignored you and so forth."

"Okay, so we understand his motives maybe.

That sure doesn't mean his damn Patchwork Man won't be able to kill you."

"I'm taking precautions."

"The same kind you took with Sentimental Sid?"

Jake ceased stroking her. "I screwed up there, with an assist from Wildcat."

"And what about Wildcat? He's liable to push his way into this whole—"

"He's got, at the minimum, another day to sleep off the Stunoleum," Jake assured her. "Before we called in Gunther's people I hid our sleeping protagonist away in an abandoned organic fruit farm on the outskirts of Monterey. We don't have to worry about him this time."

"Wildcat has a way of showing up unexpectedly."

"He won't."

Hildy shook her head, unconvinced. "What did Steranko the Siphoner want when he called?"

"Money."

"For what?"

"I'll show you when it arrives in the morning. He's faxing it out."

"Something to help you?"

"Should be," answered Jake. "Steranko tracked down a copy of a manuscript Dr. Patchwork tried to sell before he went underground. Supposedly it goes into his entire process in great detail."

She undid the seam of his tunic. "Like to make love?"

"I would."

"One last time," she said.

"Um, don't be a gloomygus," advised Corky from the floor.

Chapter 21

Dummy under his arm, Jake was standing backstage at the Vaudeville Palace in Santa Monica. He wore the familiar two-piece checked funsuit and green frightwig identified with the real Preston McGinty. The large dome theater sat at the edge of the ocean and a night wind was coming in and burring at the multicolor neoglass panels.

A bear ambled by wheeling a bike. "Everybody's in position, Jake," he confided in a low growly voice.

Jake merely nodded, continuing to watch the act which was out on the vaudeville stage.

The bear moved on.

Busino & Marcus were doing their School Daze routine, the large audience was responding enthusiastically.

"Vot's dot you got dere, lummox?"

"Dot's an apple for you, teacher."

"Vot kind uff apple got stripes on it already?"

"Okay, so maybe it was a vatermelon."

Jake shook his head. "I'll wow them if they laugh at this kind of crap."

"I know you."

Turning, he saw a pretty dark-haired girl, naked from the waist up, smiling tentatively at him. "Possible, possible, kid. McGinty & Corky are famous."

"You weren't McGinty the last time I met you I don't think." She frowned thoughtfully. "I'd swear you were in the lobby at KHOB-TV not more than a few days ago."

"McGinty & Corky don't work toilets like KHOB, kid."

"Possibly we met elsewhere. I'm the KHOB receptionist but I'm also a member of the Bellybuttons."

"Um, didn't recognize you without your sack," said the dangling Corky.

"He's cute. Are you completely certain you didn't stroll into KHOB pretending to be a Mr. Chambers from the—"

"We been here in Santa Mon doing the Vigorish Vanities for two solid weeks, sis," Jake told her, patting his wig as he did. "Did old Vigorish hire you kids?"

"Yes, this is our first night with the show. We're replacing Dynamo Daisy, better known as the Girl With The Electric Tits. Apparently she shorted out."

"Better go get into your costume," suggested Jake, pretending to be watching Marcus whap Busino over the head with a handful of celery.

"Dot'll fix you, you dodgasted bummer."

"Keep dot up, teach, and I giffs der vatermelon back to der guy I stole it from."

"Guess I will go slip into my sack," said the Bellybutton girl. "Nice meeting you again, or for the first time, as the case may be." She smiled again, went away down one of the dressing room ramps.

"Um, I thought you was a whiz at disguise, boss."

"Wouldn't think she could have seen me all that well with a bag over her."

"What the frap are they doing now?" asked a surly voice behind Jake. "What's this with the carrots?"

"If they get a big enough laugh with the celery, they do it again with carrots," Jake told the bulky magician who had come up from the dressing room area.

"They're into my time," complained the magician, with a tug at his pointed beard. "People flock to the Vigorish Vanities to see me, not low comedy. They love Breakstone the Amazing Escape Artist. Love me."

"Um, that's how stupid I am," said Corky. "I thought they came to see the girls."

"I hate ventriloquists who do that," mentioned the man called Breakstone. "Use their frapping dummies to wise off."

"I thought they came to see the girls," said Jake with a grin. "Better?"

"No time for you." The magician pushed Jake aside and before Marcus & Busino had taken their final bow he was out on the stage.

"Handsome beard he has," said Jake.

"About as real as your green hair," said the dummy.

"Yeah, but I recognized him and he didn't recognize me."

Out in the glare of the floating spotlights Breakstone had both hands held high. "No one in the world can perform this amazing escape except yours truly," he was telling the expectant audience.

"We're going out front." Jake moved through the backstage dimness.

When Breakstone requested, "May I have someone out of the audience to help me lock myself into this allegedly escape-proof casket?" Jake darted up onto the stage from the first row of seats.

"Scram," urged Breakstone as Jake and his dummy approached him and his prop casket. "I want a real sucker not a—"

"Audience loves this," Jake said.

The hundreds of people out there were laughing and applauding, having recognized what they assumed to be Preston McGinty & Corky.

"Um, I think I can be as good a stooge as the next guy," Corky said.

"This violates the ethics of show biz," protested the escape artist.

Jake grinned out at the audience. "I do believe he's afraid to let an expert lock him up. What do you folks think?"

"Boo!"

"Poor sport!"

"Do the trick!"

"Let's see some magic!"

"Breakstone fears no challenge," the magician bellowed. "Therefore, I will climb within this casket now. I ask this gentleman to make sure I am securely chained and locked in."

"We want to examine those locks," said Corky.

"Test them all, young man," Breakstone invited.

After this was done, Jake said, "They're all real, ladies and gentlemen. It will indeed require a man of amazing gifts to escape from this prison."

"I'll show you." The magician climbed into the strong metal casket, stretched out on his back. "Shut the lid, then wind the chains around and slip them—"

"Let's make it a shade tougher." Jake fished a pair of handcuffs from a pocket. "You won't have any trouble getting free of these, too, will you?"

He held the metal bracelets up so they flashed in the spotlights' glare.

"Breakstone can escape any manacle known to man." Lips pressed tight, he held out his wrists.

Jake snapped on the cuffs. "Next time you try to impersonate Breakstone get a more believable beard, Wildcat." He slammed the casket shut on the Federal Police agent.

"He wouldn't want you to do that," Jake told the silver-haired Lorenz Vigorish. "Violates the showman's code."

The small show producer was anxiously watching the chained casket, which had been dragged backstage once it had become evident Breakstone wasn't going to emerge immediately. "It violates my code to do a kafloppo like he did."

"The casket has air vents," Jake pointed out. "I know Breakstone will be terribly embarrassed if you saw him out of that before he exhausts all his options for escape, Lorenz."

"Usually he does it so easy. Tonight with a full house he does a kafloppo." Vigorish kicked the casket. "What's wrong with you, Breakstone?" He pressed an ear to the metal. "I don't even hear him struggling in there."

"He confided in me only this evening that he was trying out a new Far Eastern method of escape," Jake told the producer, who wasn't aware he was not talking to the authentic Preston McGinty. "This method involves meditation and trancelike states."

"Trances aren't good boxoffice," said Vigorish. "Okay, we'll leave him be. When he finally does get out tell him I want to have a little talk in my office about Far Eastern mysticism and kafloppos."

After the Vanities producer had strode away Corky remarked, "Um, I bet that little needle in the handcuffs had something to do with his trancelike state."

"Possibly, Corky. I'm not up on all the latest in Far Eastern techniques." With Wildcat out of the way Jake returned his full attention to playing decoy.

Jake took a third bow, tossed his dummy high in the air and caught it. Despite his continual smiling at the exuberant audience he was unhappy. He'd done his entire act plus two encores and no attempt had been made to kill him.

Backstage the Bellybuttons were frantically signalling him to get off stage and let them on.

"Didn't work," he muttered as he left the spotlights.

"What a ham, what a showboat," complained one of the Bellybuttons when he came into the wings. "You ran nine minutes over."

"Just warming them up for more ventriloquists, girls," he remarked in passing.

Jake's shoulders took on a dejected slump on the down ramp. By the time he reached his underground dressing room he was dragging his feet, carrying the dummy by one of its arms.

"A shame, Jake," said Gunther Stool. He was sitting in the wicker chair beside the makeup mirror. "Your estimable plan has failed. At least so it seems to me."

Jake's nose wrinkled, then he grinned one of his most unearthly grins. "You ought to take better care of yourself," he said to the jowly man. "You must have spilled some coquille on yourself up in

Frisco, and you still give off a faint odor of bay leaf."

"San Francisco, Jake? I haven't been up in—"

"Gunther Stool hasn't. But you have, Patchwork Man."

Chapter 22

"We've decided to add you to our stockpile," said the Patchwork Man, his features still molded into a facsimile of Gunther Stool's. This close you could see the tiny scars which remained after his assembling. A thin whitish line around the left wrist, a puckered wavy line circling the neck.

"Explosion? Electric shock?" Jake seated himself in the small dressing room's only other chair, rested Corky on his knee.

"Stalling, by the way, won't help you now, Pace. As Stool I dismissed most of the guards and security people before I came down here. How'd I know them? A cinchy task for the part of my brain I got from Hoodoo Hannigan, the late great, as you know, mind robber."

"Is that how you tumbled to the fact I wasn't Preston McGinty?"

The Patchwork Man said, "Didn't need any ESP for that, Pace. Once I espied Wildcat Brasher posing as an illusionist I knew you had to be here, too. Part of me, you may not be aware, is the recently deceased Professor Memorex, the man who never forgets a face. After I noticed Wildcat, in his not very effective disguise, I was alerted. When you intruded into his act, I realized who you were almost at once."

"Therefore you must have realized you were in a trap. Why didn't you take off?"

"I discussed that with Dr. Wolverton, via the telepathy route, and he, being a great fan and admirer of yours, saw this as a marvelous opportunity to add you to our spare parts warehouse," explained the Patchwork Man. "Yes, the doctor foresees using pieces of you in several forthcoming composites. So I altered my face, and here I am."

"What's your range when you communicate with him?"

"You're curious as to where he is? He's right out on the #2 parking lot with his skyvan."

"Our people should have noticed him."

"He's disguised as a microwave soydog vendor and his van is done over to resemble a delivery truck." The Patchwork Man laughed with Shocker Fulson's laugh. "You and that inept Wildcat are not the only disguise experts, Pace."

Jake patted the dummy's head. "Once you do me in, how are you going to get me out to Dr. Patchwork?"

"Dr. Wolverton doesn't care for that nickname, even now when his work is being recognized and he's reaping such a satisfying revenge." The composite man stood.

"Dr. Wolverton then."

"Nothing grandstandy tonight. Instead of teleking you, I'm quite simply going to drop your remains in that wardrobe trunk yonder. After redoing my face to resemble yours exactly I carry you to the truck and the doctor and I speed away into the night." He took a single step closer to Jake. "You encountered Deathwish Garfield in your now-ending career, didn't you? Yes, my Professor Memorex cells confirm that. I have the part of Deathwish's brain he used in his work. You know he was able to will a man dead. Simple, neat, unmessy." The Patchwork man rubbed his mismatched hands together. "So now I . . . Hoodoo's trying to tell me something. You're thinking something dangerous, Pace, and keeping it from me in some sneaky Tibetan mindblocking way. I warn you—"

"Dr. Wolverton wrote a book." Jake thrust his hand into the dummy's hollow back. "Told all about his work with composite men. Even outlined their weaknesses. Seems his Patchwork Men can be unassembled by exposing them to certain ultrasonic waves."

"Why would he put that in a book?"

"Vanity." He triggered on the ultrasonic gun he'd built into Corky that afternoon.

"I can still wish you . . . shock you to . . . explode your damn hide so . . ." The Patchwork Man pointed at Jake warningly. Then his fingers began to fall off. He tilted his head, watching them splat on the dressing room floor.

The head popped free of the neck. It hit against Jake's boot before rolling under the table, leaving an ear behind.

An arm fell next. Beneath the suit a leg had separated. The fragmenting body thumped and splashed to the floor, flesh tangling with cloth, bones spearing out, entrails bursting free.

Jake backed away from the pile that had been the Patchwork Man. He turned off the sonicgun and placed Corky on a shelf.

"Some finish," said the dummy.

"Get them while they last! Soydoggies! Why haven't you kept in mind contact, you buffoon?"

Dr. Patchwork, clad in a one-piece vendorsuit, was standing next to a soydog cart and pretending to solicit the few Vanities patrons who were leaving the domed playhouse.

Jake, the empty wardrobe trunk on one shoulder, said, "Pace proved to be a tough opponent. It was nip and tuck there for a spell."

"Dump him in the van and we'll be off for Anaheim," said the doctor. "We may use Pace's parts to build the new team of improved Patchwork Men. The ones I intend to use to take control of the Ladies Mafia away from that dippy Fancy Dawntreader once she's established it. I've been ignored and maligned too long by the so-called powers that be and now, since fate has seen fit to send me a little capital, my day is dawning. Keep a man of genius on the outside looking in, my friends, and I warn you, he will one fine day break in! Yes, into your highclass parlors and your—"

"Is that real sauerkraut?"

"What?"

"In your cart there. That would go good right about now. A soydog with real sauerkraut." Jake set the trunk down.

"Sauerkraut? I stand on the threshold of world fame and you . . . what part of your brain are you using to think about sauerkraut?"

"The same old Jake Pace part, Dr. Patchwork."

"You're not supposed to . . . oops."

"Exactly." Jake took a stungun from his tunic. "Afraid your climb to greatness ends right about here."

"You do a very good impression of a Patchwork Man doing an impression of you, down to those very believable scars," said the rumpled doctor.

"It's a shame I won't get to chop you up into spare parts."

"That it is," said Jake.

Twangy guitar music was flowing out of the pixphone.

"Well, thanks." Jake had one foot edging out of their phone alcove. "I think you've adopted the exactly right attitude. Sure, goodbye."

Hildy came walking into the living room of their West Redding home. "Who was that?"

"The president," replied her husband. "He phoned to tell us he appreciated our cleaning up the Patchwork business, even though it meant prison for his favorite show biz personality. He even played me a few strains of his old hit, *Happy As A Hound Dog In Heat*."

"But he took Fancy's arrest fairly hard, didn't he?"

"At one point there were tears in his eyes."

"If I played guitar as badly as he does I'd cry, too." Hildy went over to watch the twilight.

"Ramblin' Billy, despite your opinions of his musical gifts, sends you his best. He's pleased with the way we handled this one."

"We?"

Jake approached her. "Do I sense a sulk?"

"Not at all." Hildy directed her words at the window. "It's only that you insisted on my keeping out of the final phase, insisted on playing decoy all alone and then went out and caught Dr. Patchwork singlehanded."

"You impersonated Fancy, I impersonated a ventriloquist. Both parts of the strategy were equally important. How would you like to go to Tahiti?"

She faced him, an eyebrow raised. "Do we have a new job?"

"Nope. I feel the need of a vacation," said Jake. "If we go right now we'll be in time for the Tahiti Film Festival."

"I'll pack," said Hildy.

"In awhile," said Jake.

BOOKS

If you really only want the best in Science Fiction and Fantasy, these are the blockbusters you cannot afford to miss!

☐ **HUNTER OF WORLDS** by C. J. Cherryh. Triple fetters of the mind served to keep their human prey in bondage to this city-sized starship. (#UE1314—$1.75)

☐ **THE REALMS OF TARTARUS** by Brian M. Stableford. Three novels in one make up this unprecedented saga of the world divided between heaven above and hell below. (#UJ1309—$1.95)

☐ **THE GAMEPLAYERS OF ZAN** by M. A. Foster. The final showdown between a quasi-superrace and their all-too-human creators. (#UJ1287—$1.95)

☐ **THE FORBIDDEN TOWER** by Marion Zimmer Bradley. A Darkover novel of the power of group-love versus the austerity of the matrix acolytes. (#UJ1323—$1.95)

☐ **THE WORLD ASUNDER** by Ian Wallace. They were prepared to shatter the Earth itself to thwart the rise of a cosmic tyrant. (#UW1262—$1.50)

DAW BOOKS are represented by the Publishers of Signet and Mentor Books, THE NEW AMERICAN LIBRARY, INC.
